NEVER WALK ALONE

WILLOW ROSE

Walk on through the wind
Walk on through the rain
Though your dreams be tossed and blown

Walk on, walk on
With hope in your heart
And you'll never walk alone

Gerry & The Pacemakers, 1963

Chapter 1

"THE STREETS ARE COMPLETELY EMPTY. It's eerie."

Candice looked out the window. She pulled the curtain aside with a finger.

"No cars, no one walking on the pavement. There isn't even a siren sounding in all of Miami."

Candice sniffled into the phone. Bryan hadn't said anything for quite a while, and she wondered if he was all right. She lifted her gaze and found his from the building next to hers. He was standing in his window, looking back at her, waving casually. She placed a hand on the glass with a deep sigh.

If only she could feel his touch.

"Did you do something to your hair?" he asked.

She blushed and ran her fingers through it. She had done something different this morning. Usually, she'd keep it in a ponytail, as she had for the entire two weeks she had been in isolation in her small condo. Just like she had barely cared to shower. Why would she? She was a single woman living in Miami. She wasn't going to see anyone for a very long time. Not since they blocked off the streets and told them all to stay inside.

So far, no one knew how long this was going to last—indefinitely sounded so scary. She couldn't help wondering if she would ever be able to leave the condo again. And that had given her many panic attacks in the beginning. She could feel her heart rate go up just from thinking about it, and she could sit in her living room just staring at the door, wondering if she'd ever get to open it again. Of course, she would, she kept telling herself. They were, after all, allowed to go to the grocery store and shop, even though they only let five people in at a time, to make sure they didn't get too close to each other. Candice had only gone out twice since they were put on lockdown. In the beginning, she had watched the news constantly, but that just made her even more scared, so now she didn't even open social media anymore. She read lots of books and watched Netflix until she wanted to throw up. She did yoga in her living room and looked out the window at the empty street below while wondering how things had gone so wrong. The theories were many if you asked people online.

Was it nature trying to take the planet back? Was it God's punishment on the human race for living the sinful lives they did? That's what her friend, Loretta, seemed to believe. She was annoying, but she was also the only friend who called her every now and then. It happened more frequently now, and there was no escaping that call no matter how much she wanted to. Candice couldn't really tell her that she was too busy. Busy doing what? She'd only ask. No one was busy these days, not since everything had come to a sudden stop. Life as they knew it had come to a halt.

"Yes, I straightened it and left it down," Candice said into the phone, touching her hair again. "Do you like it?"

Bryan smiled behind his window in the building across from hers. He had such kind eyes.

"I love it. It looks amazing."

"Did you shave?" she asked with a grin.

"Why, yes, I did. I wanted to look good for you today. I know it's silly, but right now, your calls are the highlight of my day."

He laughed after saying it, but it didn't sound happy. She knew how he felt. It was the same emotion that went through her. Just two weeks ago, they had lived normal lives, and they hadn't even known that each other existed. They had each been so busy with their own lives, careers, and friends that they had never even looked out the window and seen one another.

After three days in isolation, their eyes had met all of a sudden. He had waved cautiously, and she had waved back, happy to see another human being. This continued for a few more days, till one day he held up a sign with a phone number written on it. She had grabbed her phone, then called him, and now they met this way every day. They had never met face to face; they had never held hands or kissed. Yet Candice felt like she was falling in love with him, and she sensed that he felt the same. Maybe it was just the situation, but she had never felt like this before. They could talk for hours on end. Sometimes, they'd listen to music together. He had an old-fashioned record player, and he'd play her a song, and then they'd listen and talk about it afterward. Yesterday, he had even recited a poem for her, one he had written himself, just for her, he said. Today, he had told her how he couldn't wait to take her out once this was all over. Candice could hardly wait either. She liked Bryan more than any of the men she had dated on Tinder, and there were a lot of those. There was something so pure and simple about their relationship if you

3

could call it that. It was just easy, and as people were realizing in their solitude what was really important in life, she was wondering if she had prioritized things wrong as well. Candice had been shooting up the career ladder all her adult life, and she had barely allowed herself any time for love.

A casual date here and there had often ended in just as casual sex where she told the guy to leave once it was done. She hated it if they asked to sleep over and kicked them out as soon as daylight came knocking. No breakfast, no kiss goodbye. She had liked her solitude; being alone kept her mind clear and focused. Now, she'd do anything to break that silence and get rid of the deep loneliness gnawing at her. Sometimes, she wanted to scream, or just run out into the street, hugging anyone she might meet. She had no idea how badly loneliness hurt the body, how terribly you could miss something as simple as a hug. How the body almost craved physical contact after a few weeks in solitude.

Candice felt a tear escape her eye and wiped it away. Bryan couldn't see it from where he was standing, but she had a feeling he shed a tear every now and then as well. It was wearing on everyone being cooped up like this.

"So, what are you having for dinner tonight?" he asked.

"I made a vegan casserole," she sniffled, pressing back the sad thoughts. They weren't doing her any good.

She glanced toward the stove. Candice had been cooking like crazy ever since the lockdown started. Just to have something to do to keep her sanity. Before this, she never cooked. She didn't have the time or energy for it once she got home late at night from work, and would usually order in. But now, it was the most important task of the day. Every day, a new recipe, trying to eat healthily and just having something sensible to do. In the beginning, she had found herself going to the store just for a gallon of milk or a chocolate bar, just in the desire to be able to get out. But since then, they had put restrictions on how many times a week you were allowed to leave your house, and for a single woman like her, it was down to once a week. To stop the virus from spreading, they kept saying. To flatten the curve, to prevent people from overwhelming the hospitals. It all made sense, and Candice understood the reasons, but still. It was hard to keep the optimism going.

"Ah, I wish I could taste it. I bet it is awesome," Bryan said.

"I wish I could have you over. We could eat and share a glass of wine."

"That would be awesome."

A silence broke out between them as they both remembered what it was like, how life used to be. Back to a time —two weeks ago—when you could actually invite people over for dinner or go out to a nice restaurant and eat together.

"What are you having tonight?"

"Just leftover chicken from yesterday. I made a salad to go with it, though. Trying to stay healthy."

"Don't forget to take your vitamins too," she said, sounding a little too much like a mother warning her child. "Even though they don't know if it helps, it can't harm boosting the immune system."

"I'm not scared of this virus," he said. "It's nothing but a bad cold, right?"

Candice swallowed. She didn't want to talk about this with him or anyone. But she felt she needed to warn him.

"It's not, no."

"But that's what they say on TV. It's not that bad. It's a flu-like disease that affects children and young adults the worst. That's why we need to stay inside because we need to protect the kids. But for most people, it's like the common cold."

It's not true. It's way worse than that. They don't know what they're up against yet.

She wanted to say that, but she couldn't.

"Just stay inside," she said instead. "And wear gloves and a mask if you go to the store. Please."

He cleared his throat in the phone. "Of course. I'm not dumb."

Oh, no, I made him mad.

"I didn't say that; sorry, Bryan. It's just…well, this virus terrifies me to the core."

"I know. Lots of people are scared," he said. "But I think they're exaggerating. We'll be fine. Just wait and see."

Candice felt her eyes grow moist. She stifled the tears, then nodded and looked at Bryan, wondering if she'd ever get to meet him. How could life be so cruel that once she finally found someone she might love, once she finally got her priorities right and realized what was really important, the world was about to run out of time?

Chapter 2

BRYAN HARPER PUT the phone down as Candice hung up, promising she'd call him later so they could watch the Netflix show *The Tiger King* together. He didn't care much for that particular show, but it seemed to be all everyone was talking about, so he had given it a chance, watching it every night with her. Candice didn't like it either, she said, but it gave them something to talk about and a sort of common ground. They could laugh at the characters together, at how ridiculous they were, and he kind of liked that. Candice was a smart woman, he had realized. She was well educated; you could tell by the way she talked. She hadn't told him what she did for a living before all this started, but he got a feeling it was something that needed an awful lot of education. Bryan was a teacher and did online school with his sixth-grade students every day. He was lucky, he guessed since he didn't risk losing his job. Many of his friends had been fired right when the entire country shut down at once, and they knew more were to come. Many had just taken pay cuts so far, but since they didn't know how long this was going to last, more would lose their jobs sooner rather than later. The world was a mess, he felt, but he still kept a sense of optimism and told himself life would go back to normal at some point. Of course, it would. Or at least some kind of normal, a new normal, maybe. He didn't share his friends' and colleagues' pessimism when looking at the future. At least not anymore. Because now, he really had something to look forward to. He'd get to see Candice in real life and hold her in his arms, and he couldn't wait for that. They'd be able to go on a real date, and what a story they'd have to tell their grandchildren one day. Being on lockdown had made Bryan realize he was lonely and that he never wanted to walk through life alone again after this. He just prayed she'd still like him when she met him face to face. He didn't know if it was just the loneliness making her attracted to him because there was no one else right at this moment. That's not how he felt about her. He thought she was the most beautiful woman he had ever seen, and he couldn't believe they had been living so close for years and didn't even know each other. How had they never seen one another through the windows?

Bryan looked after her as she disappeared from her position, and he imagined her going to the kitchen, finishing her casserole. He couldn't see her when she was in her kitchen, but as soon as she was back in the living room, he would look at her again. He hadn't told her this, but he looked at her a lot. He couldn't help himself and hoped she wouldn't think he was a creep. It was just because he missed her so much as soon as they hung up. He would sit in his living room and watch her over there as she went about her day, especially when she did her yoga every morning. He enjoyed that a lot. Did that make him a pervert? He hoped not.

His cat, Lora, jumped up in the windowsill and

meowed. He petted her back gently. "I am not forgetting about you, Lora. You'll always be my favorite girl. How about we grab something to eat too, huh? I see Candice is sitting down and having her dinner now."

He sighed as he watched her sit down at her dining room table and dig in. How he wished he could sit there with her and enjoy something as simple as a meal. He wondered if she was a loud chewer or if she was one of those quiet women afraid of making a noise—how he would give his right arm to know this or even just to be able to touch her skin. How did she feel? Was she soft? He was certain she was. Candice was the type who took good care of herself.

Bryan walked to the fridge and pulled out the chicken from the night before, then microwaved it and pulled out a bag of salad, then put some dressing on and placed it on the plate. He wished he liked to cook the way Candice seemed to enjoy it. Then he could come up with some more interesting dishes than chicken three nights in a row, followed by spaghetti and meatballs for yet another three days. They were the only two dishes he knew how to cook.

Bryan sat down and glanced at Candice, who was chewing while scrolling on her phone, probably going through work emails or maybe watching the news, even though she had told him she had stopped since it made her so depressed. All those awful images from the filled-up hospitals in Miami scared him as well, even though he pretended they didn't. Miami was the epicenter, they said. It was here it had all started. But after a week, it had spread to the rest of the country, and soon after, the rest of the world too. They had closed Miami down and then the rest of the state of Florida, but it was too late. The world was closing down a few days later. All planes were grounded, schools shut down, and soon there was a stay at home order from the president. It all went by so fast; Bryan hadn't even been able to visit his mother at the nursing home outside of Miami. His sister lived across town, too, and had two young children. He just prayed they weren't hit. Jane had called a few hours earlier and said that her youngest, Fiona, had come down with a fever and for him to pray that it was something else and not the virus.

Bryan lifted his beer and saluted Candice when he realized she was looking at him as well. She smiled and raised her glass of wine. They pretended to be clinking glasses when suddenly, she was interrupted. She looked at him, then at the door before she put the glass down. She glanced toward him, a puzzled look on her face.

"What's going on?" he said out into the living room, signaling to her that he didn't understand, reaching his arms in the air.

She shrugged, but then looked toward the door again before she got up.

Bryan wrinkled his forehead in concern. Was someone at her door? How was that even possible these days? Who went outside? Who knocked on someone's door?

He got up, too, and followed her every move as she walked toward her front door. Bryan hurried to the window and watched as she grabbed the lock and turned it. A sense of alarm rushed through him.

"Wait a minute," he said as if she could hear him. "Ask who it is first. Use the chain. Keep the chain on, Candice."

Bryan held his breath. He could tell she was looking through the peephole and talking through the door, doing exactly what he had said. Now, she opened the door, keeping the chain on.

"Good girl," he mumbled. "Playing it safe in these strange times is smart."

The door came ajar, and he could tell she was speaking to the person on the other side.

Probably just a neighbor wanting to borrow eggs or milk or something like that.

Bryan bit the side of his cheek as he watched her speak, and then she closed the door, and his shoulders came down, thinking it was over. The person had left. Candice couldn't get infected this way. She had stayed behind the door. She would be fine.

It was nothing.

He breathed in relief when the door suddenly was pushed in with a violent force, slamming Candice back against the wall. Stunned at this, Bryan watched as a man stepped inside and, with a quick movement, closed the door behind him. Candice had fallen, and he could tell by her open mouth that she was screaming.

ONE WEEK LATER

Chapter 3

FOR A LONG TIME, there was nothing but a rhythmic buzz from the ventilator next to her. It was so quiet in the room that, at first, Reese believed she had, in fact, died. Right when she shot her eyes open, that's what she thought. She blinked her eyes rapidly as she scanned room 228.

But then someone showed up. It was hard to tell if it was a woman or a man till she came up close, and Reese could see the eyes inside the hazmat suit. The eyes revealed that the woman inside was smiling by the way they grew narrow and fine lines emerged at the sides.

"Am I in Hell?" Reese asked.

The nurse laughed quietly inside her suit, but then grew serious. "You're alive. But hell is probably a close description to the state of things right now. Let me go get the doctor."

She came back a short while later with the doctor, who was also wearing a yellow hazmat suit.

"How are you feeling?" the doctor asked and looked at the monitors.

"I...I don't know. Where am I?"

The doctor sighed deeply when an alarm went off from somewhere else. His eyes met those of the nurse.

"I'll fill her in," she said. "You go."

The doctor took off, almost sprinting down the hallway. Seeing this made Reese worry.

"Where...where is he going?"

"Another patient just went into cardiac arrest, I'm afraid. It's the seventh today."

Reese's eyes grew wide when hearing this.

"What's going on?"

"You've been gone for a while," the nurse said. "You've been in an induced coma for four weeks, so you don't know. Yesterday, the doctors believed you were improving, so they decided to get you off the ventilator and out of the coma. But a lot has happened in the four weeks you were out. Quite a lot, to be honest."

"I...I'm sick?" Reese asked.

The nurse nodded. "Yes. You were. You're better now. We need to run a couple more tests, but it seems like you beat this thing. You had double pneumonia along with the virus, and it almost killed you."

"Virus?"

"Oh, I forgot. You've been out, so you haven't heard. There's a virus that has placed everything on lockdown. It goes by several names. The Florida Flu or the Miami Virus. They gave it those names because it is believed to have originated here in Miami."

Reese swallowed. She felt confused.

"So...you're telling me there's some virus here in Miami?"

The nurse nodded. "Yes. I know it's a lot to take in right now, and the doctor told me to take it easy on you, break it to you gently, so you won't get overwhelmed. You can rest now if you like, then I'll come back later, and we can talk more. Unfortunately, we're really pressed for time and space these days as more and more patients roll in, so I fear that there won't be much time."

"But...wait...you're telling me the entire town is on lockdown because of this?"

She nodded. "Not just the town. The world. People have been told to stay at home. Schools are closed, restaurants are shut down, all sports events are canceled, concerts too. People are told to work from home, and only essential workers get to leave, like us, nurses and doctors, and people working in grocery stores. They don't know how long it'll last. They're only allowed to leave if they need to get medicine or food, and even for that, most people are only allowed to go out once a week and only one person from each household. It's a mess. In here, we're struggling to fit all the patients, and we don't have enough equipment to deal with this. It hits the youngest the hardest, and we're struggling to save the kids."

"But...but where did it come from?" Reese asked, feeling anxiety grow in her chest. She was in her forties, so maybe that was why she had survived? But what about the children? The horror of this was unbearable.

The nurse sighed. Another alarm went off, and Reese could tell she was about to leave when she reached out and grabbed her suit.

"Please, tell me. Do they know where the virus came from?"

The nurse paused and exhaled. "They were kind of hoping you could help them figure that out."

"Me? How so?"

"Because you were patient zero. You were the first known patient to get it."

Chapter 4

"WHAT IF I just don't do it?"

My fourteen-year-old-daughter looked up at me from behind the computer screen, leaned back in her chair, and crossed her arms in front of her chest, reminding me of when she was a lot younger and refused to do something I told her to.

"Then I guess you'll get a bad grade on it," I said with an exhale.

Homeschooling due to the lockdown had proved to be a lot harder than I expected. Usually, my daughter was very independent and could take care of things like this almost on her own. But being stuck inside and not being able to see any of her friends had made her angry at the world, and she liked to take that out on me. I knew it was just because she was actually feeling anxious. I guess we all were scared, living through something like this. The biggest question of all being, will this ever end?

Of course, we feared the virus, too; I most certainly feared Josie getting it. With her history of heart disease, she was in the high-risk group. That's why we had kept her indoors for the past four weeks. My dad had moved in with us, so he could keep an eye on her while I went to work. As a detective, I was essential and had to go out in the streets and make sure people were safe, even if it meant me risking bringing the virus home with me.

My girlfriend Jean was working non-stop at the ER, and we had decided not to see one another while this was going on, to minimize the risk of infection for Josie. But it was tough. Four weeks without being able to kiss the one you loved was no fun at all. Especially not when you had finally found one another and hadn't gotten to date for more than a few weeks when the entire world suddenly went crazy.

The past few weeks had been insane. It was hard to wrap my mind around it.

"What does it matter if I get a bad grade on it? What do grades matter anyway?" Josie asked. "It's not like we're going back to school. I might even not survive this if I get it, so why would I spend my last time on earth doing math?"

"Because you might actually survive it, and you might actually go back to school in a few weeks when they find a cure or a vaccine for this, and then you'll end the year with bad grades."

I said this, but I didn't mean it. The fact was, the girl was right. We all knew she probably wouldn't get to go back to school this year at all. And it seemed so futile to be concentrating on schoolwork when it felt like the entire world was ending. But we had to believe there was something at the end of this, that we'd make it out of this alive. We had to believe that it would all blow over at some point.

We have to believe that God knows what He's doing, even when we can't see it, even if it makes no sense.

"Please, Josie," I said and rubbed my stubble. I hadn't

shaved in several days since I had been off the entire weekend. I reminded myself to get it done before reporting for duty later today. "Please, just do the math work, and then you can take the rest of the day off. We can do the science stuff tomorrow if you want. It's not due till next Monday."

Josie stared at me defiantly. But behind all that anger, I saw something else. I saw a sadness I hardly recognized in my usually so happy little girl. She was scared. It was obvious to me, her father, even though she tried her hardest to hide it from me. I couldn't blame her. Only a month ago, she had seen her mother being taken away to enter the witness protection program and told she'd never get to see her again.

And now this?

Why, God? Why do all these terrible things happen to us? Why can't we catch a break?

My dad entered the living room just as I shook my head, not knowing what to do about my daughter. I felt his hand on my shoulder. "Here. Let me take over. You need to get ready for work anyway."

I nodded, realizing that was why Josie was extra defiant today. Because I was going back to work after two days at home, she was worried about me; of course, she was. She was anxious about everything these days and had no way of putting her anxiety into words. Instead, she became like a toddler, refusing to obey.

"I might as well save you the trouble right away. It doesn't matter what you say. I'm not doing it, Grandpa," she said. "I don't want to waste any more time on school."

My dad sat down, and I got up. I was about to walk away when my dad folded his hands in front of him and nodded.

"Okay," he said. "So, don't."

I paused. That wasn't exactly what I wanted to hear.

He was supposed to convince her to do her math, not the opposite.

"Dad, I…" I said, but he lifted his finger in the air to stop me. I backed off, deciding to let him deal with it. I had given it my best; if he believed he could do better, then I might as well let him try.

I walked upstairs and took a shower, then shaved and got dressed. I placed my gun in the holster and attached my badge to the belt. I looked at myself in the mirror, then glanced toward Jean's house next door. It was empty, and she was probably at work, as usual these days. She only came home to sleep for a few hours before she was off again. If she even came home at all. I missed her terribly. I missed her kisses, holding her hand, and just smelling her skin. I missed her cooking and the sound of her voice. I missed everything about her, and it filled me with such deep sadness that I had no idea when I'd really be able to be with her again.

I walked down the stairs and found Josie sitting at the computer, working. I came up behind her and looked at the screen, then realized she was actually doing her math problems. My dad was in the kitchen, emptying the dishwasher and humming. I walked out to him and gave him a look.

"Okay. How did you do it?"

"That's between Josie and me," he said grinning.

"Spit out, Dad. How did you do it?"

He laughed. "I might have promised her a new game for her Nintendo Switch if she finished her work before this afternoon. There's this game she's been asking for for a long time, but you keep telling her it's too expensive. Animal Cropping or something."

"Crossing. Animal Crossing," I said, startled at what I was hearing. My dad was a retired pastor; I had expected him to have a chat with her about how God was using all this to turn people to Him, or maybe how God saw her good deeds, and she'd be rewarded for it later on. Not this.

"You can't bribe her."

My dad gave me a puzzled look. "Why not? It worked. Look at her."

"Yes, it worked…for now. But what about tomorrow? She's gonna expect to get something every time she finishes some work, and I can't afford that. You know I can't. Neither can you. You're not exactly swimming in money either."

"True. But sometimes they need to have something to look forward to. Desperate times call for desperate measures. And these times sure are desperate."

I scoffed and took my phone from the counter.

"I don't know what I am ever going to do with you. Both of you."

Chapter 5

REESE HADN'T HAD a minute to herself ever since she woke up from her coma. The next couple of days seemed like a dream—a nightmare mostly. There wasn't even a second to think about what was going on or what had happened to her. It was all chaos around her. There was a constant stream of people coming in and out of her room. Some were asking her questions, while others rushed in to take blood, take her temperature, or run other tests. Two men from the CDC arrived and told her they were performing what they called contact tracing, then asked her a ton of questions, none of which she knew the answer to.

"Where were you before you ended up in the hospital?"

"Who were you in contact with?"

"Did you travel before contracting the virus?"

Reese just stared at them, eyes wide, mouth gaping. She was scared. All these eyes looking out at her from behind their hazmat suits. They all wanted something, but she wasn't sure she could give it to them. From inside their suits, their voices

21

sounded distorted like they were further away than they actually were. Reese struggled to think and felt like she was on trial. She felt sweaty and anxious. How could she explain to them that she didn't know anything? Would they believe her when she told them that she simply didn't remember a single thing of what happened before she ended up in the hospital?

"Please, ma'am, please try to answer our questions. Did you visit family?"

"I don't think so."

"Did you have contact with any children?"

"I don't know. I don't recall."

"Okay, let's try a different approach. What is the last thing you remember?"

Reese paused and thought it over for a second. What did she remember, if anything at all? A vision came to her, an image of her in her condo, in the bed. And she wasn't alone. She was with someone; there was a voice there, another voice. But she couldn't put a face to it.

She felt like screaming.

Why is everything spinning so terribly fast?

Reese couldn't focus; she couldn't picture who was with her in the bed, and that was it. The image went away.

"I…I just remember being at home," she said. "I don't even remember falling ill."

"And before you were at your home?" the man asked.

Reese looked at her fingers. She didn't know what to tell him.

"I have never…my memory isn't very good," she said. "All I know is what they told me here…that I got sick in a grocery store."

"Please, do try and remember," the man said impatiently. "It's important."

Reese bit her lip and shook her head. "I'm sorry."

"We spoke to your manager where you work, at the CVS on Biscayne Boulevard, and they said you didn't come in for your shift on the twenty-second of last month. You were there the day before but seemed out of it, he said. You were babbling and sweating and coughing. So, he sent you home. Do you know if you went directly home after that? Or did you have contact with anyone while you were sick and possibly contagious?"

"I...I don't think so." She lied because now she just wanted to be left alone. This was a lot to take in, especially since she was beginning to understand that they believed she was the one who had started it all.

It all began with her—patient zero.

"You don't think so, or do you know for sure?" the man in the hazmat suit asked.

She shook her head. "No. I went straight home when they told me to."

"And you live alone? Am I correct?"

She nodded. "Yes."

She wasn't even sure about that part. She had partners from time to time. Some stayed a long time, while others only lasted a few days.

"Did you have contact with anyone in your building? A neighbor, a friend? Any children?"

She shook her head again, even though she didn't know. She simply didn't remember anything from those days. It was all blacked out except that image of her in the bed, and the sound of someone crying.

"And you're sure about this?"

She nodded and closed her eyes. As the men finally gave up and left, Reese pressed back the tears as they emerged. Two nurses came rushing into her room.

"We need you out of here. We need your space for

more severely ill patients. We're running out of room and ventilators."

She looked up at them. She could still barely walk after weeks in a coma, and now they were throwing her out?

"But...but where do I go? What if I infect more people?"

"Your latest tests came back negative," the nurse said. She was speaking rapidly, almost swallowing the words before they even left her lips. Reese could see in her eyes that she was stressed. Still, she did her best to explain it to Reese, to make sure she understood. "That means there's no more virus in your body. You're out of the loop. You can't infect more people. Many more are getting sick out there and coming in here. Since we don't have any available beds anymore, we're discharging you."

Reese stared at her, unable to speak. She was still weak and tired and hardly had any time to digest what had happened. She had only been awake for two days and was still coughing and wheezing when she breathed. But apparently, it wasn't enough anymore. They handed her a bag of pills, told her they had called for a taxi to take her home, then rolled her out of the ICU in a wheelchair. They stopped in the lobby, just as an ambulance rolled up, and another patient was taken in on a stretcher. The nurses didn't even say goodbye to Reese; they just left her there, then took off after the stretcher.

Reese rose to her feet and leaned against the wall for support. Breathing heavily, she staggered out the sliding doors, out into the unusually fresh Miami air, to a city where everything stood completely still. Except for the ambulances that were rushing in and out of the hospital, unloading patients before driving down the streets to pick up more that had fallen ill.

Chapter 6

WE WERE DRIVING through the deserted city of Miami, my partner and me. Each of us, of course, driving in our own car, complying with the strict social distancing rules for our nation. We had just been going through Overtown, the worst part of town where people usually hang on corners, dealing crack, and found that to be deserted as well as the rest of the city. Not a single soul was in the streets. Not even a deal going on in a corner or an alley.

We turned around the building housing the University of Miami's facility, where the drug addicts usually could exchange their used needles for new ones to stop the spread of HIV and hepatitis among them. But even that was closed these days, leaving the drug addicts to reuse old ones or share needles, endangering themselves.

I grabbed my radio and told my new partner, Detective Propper, that I was making a stop because I spotted someone on the street. He was sitting in a rusty beach chair that he probably pulled out of a dumpster somewhere.

"I'll only be a minute," I said and got out, grabbing my

brown bag with my lunch in hand. I pulled up my mask that the city made us wear to prevent us from getting infected when talking to people.

"If it isn't Detective Hunter," the man in the chair grinned. "To what do I owe the honor?"

"Old Man Jones," I said. "Just checking in. How're you holding up? You staying safe? Keeping your distance?"

"Ain't no one coming close to me," he said, laughing. "Weren't before the world went mad, and most certainly aren't now."

"That's good," I said. "You better keep at least six feet from everyone these days."

Social distancing was hard on the homeless, especially those that lived in the shelters where they slept in close quarters. It wasn't easy for people with no home to be asked to stay at home. I had known Old Man Jones for years, ever since he ended up on the streets. Due to cancer, he lost his job a couple of years back, and as the medical bills piled up, he could no longer afford a home, so he took to the streets. He wasn't an addict and usually hung out at the library during the day and spent the nights at one of the city's homeless shelters. Now, the library was closed, and the shelters no longer allowed for them to drop in and shower or even wash their hands. He didn't dare to sleep at the shelters anymore due to how close they slept, he had told me recently.

"If one of them has the virus, I'm done for," he said. "Better off out here in the fresh air."

And he was right about that. But being on the street at night was also dangerous, and I worried something was going to happen to him. I was especially worried that he might get the virus since his immune system was weak due to cancer.

"You get anything to eat today?" I asked.

He looked up at me. He didn't have to answer. I could tell by the look in his eyes. Most of the soup kitchens had closed because no volunteers showed up, and the people living on the streets went hungry. When cheap fast food businesses closed, there was nowhere they could go to the bathroom or wash their hands either.

I nodded. "Thought so. Here you go."

I handed him the brown bag with my lunch that my dad had made for me. Old Man Jones stared up at me.

"I'm not taking no for an answer," I said. "Take it."

He grabbed it with both hands. I saw a tear in the corner of his eye but pretended not to. I also handed him a small travel-size bottle of hand sanitizer. He gave me another grateful look.

"I gotta go. My partner is waiting. We have work to do. Stay out of trouble," I said.

"The world is ending. What kind of trouble could I possibly get myself in that is worse than this?" he yelled after me with another grin.

I rushed back, then got in my car.

"What was that all about?" Propper asked over the radio as we took off. "You do realize you risk getting the virus by talking to that guy, don't you? And that bottle of hand sanitizer? There's a lack of that stuff everywhere; these things are impossible to come by and are sold for a hundred bucks on eBay. You just handed him the entire bottle? What if you need it later today? Or tomorrow? You can't buy them anywhere."

"God will supply what I need," I said. "You can't out-give God."

Propper scoffed. "So, you're saying that if I go around giving away stuff, I can just ask God for more, and he'll give it to me?"

I nodded. "That is exactly how it works, yes."

Propper laughed into the radio, mocking me. "Gosh, you are naïve. You are a kind man, Hunter, I give you that, but you are also stupid, risking your life like this. A lot of the homeless carry the virus. They're a disaster waiting to happen. And once they start dying in the streets, not even that God of yours can save them. The way I see it, your faith is a pillow that makes you ignorant of how serious it really is, and that is dangerous. When people start relying on their gods and not science, that's when we get in real trouble."

I ignored my partner with a small smile. He was a work in progress; I knew that much. Plus, I was used to my colleagues mocking me for my faith. That didn't hurt me. I knew my God would provide for me even in these uncertain times. He had moved huge mountains in my life before, and he wasn't going to stop now.

Chapter 7

WE HAD MADE it halfway through town when my phone rang. I looked at the display. It said Bryan Harper on the screen, and I sighed, then spoke into the radio.

"It's him again."

"You're the one who gave him your cell number," Propper laughed. "I keep telling you this, but you're too kind. I would never give a witness my cell number. This is what you get."

"What do I tell him?" I asked and pulled my car to the side of the road. "I don't have anything new."

Doing detective work wasn't easy during this time of being on lockdown. Even though the workload was significantly smaller, the few cases we had were hard to investigate, since it involved a lot of talking to people. Instead, we had to interview people over the phone, and it was hard to tell if someone was lying to you when you couldn't see their face, or even use any of your normal instincts when observing people during interviews.

Bryan Harper claimed he had witnessed a girl being attacked in her apartment in the building across from his.

This was a week ago, and we had no idea what had happened to her, or if she was even the victim of a crime. We had gone to the apartment and found it empty, the door unlocked. Nothing inside the apartment indicated she had been hurt in any way, though.

To be honest, I didn't know what to tell the guy.

"Hi there, Bryan," I said, finally picking up.

"Detective Hunter? I'm just calling to check if you have any news?"

"I'm afraid not," I said. "I take it you haven't heard from her?"

"No," he said, his voice breaking. It was a strange story since at first, I got the feeling that they were in love until Bryan had told me that they had never met face to face and therefore, he didn't know any of her relatives. She had a fairly common last name, actually the single-most common name in the state of Florida, Smith, and I hadn't found any relatives that were a match. I had contacted a few Smiths in the Miami area, but none of them were related to the girl. We had her phone and computer, but none of her passwords and our computer forensics department was running low on people due to the virus, so they'd only take care of it if it were an emergency. Since we didn't have a body, a crime scene, or even evidence that the girl had been attacked, I could hardly call it that.

"I'm worried. I keep thinking about that guy that came to her door, and how he...he was so violent, pushing the door open and then he...he just dragged her out of there. Have you found the car? Remember, I told you he took her away in his car that was parked on the street?"

"Yes, the black Chevrolet with the letters LH in the license plate. No, we haven't been able to locate it yet."

"He kidnapped her. He just burst in there and took her, and I couldn't do anything," Bryan said.

I nodded, feeling sorry for the guy. I could tell he was in distress, but it was the same thing every time he called. I had no news, and he'd tell me everything again.

"And you're absolutely sure she didn't go with him voluntarily?" I asked. I knew what this guy had told me before; I knew what he saw, but we had debated whether or not he might have just thought he saw something. Propper was certain he had just imagined it or made it all up for attention. Meanwhile, I kept telling him I didn't believe that. I knew deep in my heart that something was off with this story. I just wished I could be able to sit down face to face with this Bryan person when he told us these things. It was impossible to get a real feel for his state of mind over the phone. But one thing that did speak for his story was the fact that we had found her phone in the apartment. It was left on the kitchen counter. So was her purse, along with her keys and credit cards inside of it. It was odd to leave all your belongings behind like that. Yet, no one seemed to be missing her; no family had reported it. And since there was no evidence of foul play anywhere in the apartment, that meant I was the only one in the entire precinct who took this guy remotely seriously.

"I saw her be attacked," Bryan said. "She was unconscious when he took her out of there. I'm certain of it. She didn't move. He carried her out of there, her arm over his shoulder, but he was dragging her. I called the police right after I saw him burst inside the apartment, but by the time they arrived, it was too late. He had left with her in the car. She's been gone a week now, and I fear something awful happened to her. This morning, as I woke up, I remembered something that I didn't the last time we spoke."

"And that is?"

"She had a brother. She mentioned once that she had a brother. Maybe he will know something?"

"Did she give you a name?" I asked.

"His name is Robert or Bobby. Bobby Kay Smith."

"As in *the* Bobby Kay?" I asked startled.

"Yes. She never told me his name, but she told me who he was. It's him."

Chapter 8

SHE KNEW SHE WAS BLINDFOLDED. She didn't know much else. She didn't know where she was or even what · time of day it was. Night and day became a blur in her darkness. And worst of all, she didn't know how long she would have to sit there, arms tied behind her back, legs tied together, unable to move.

Candice had tried to keep track of the days and figured she had been living about a week in complete darkness so far, unable to see anything but small rays of light peeking in underneath the cloth wrapped around her eyes, covering her sight. She knew there was a gun; her captor had a gun. She had felt it pressed against her head more than once when he spoke to her and told her to calm down and stop screaming.

"What do you want?" she asked now as her gag was removed. She spat between words to get that awful taste out of her mouth. It was always the first thing she asked him every time he removed her gag to help her drink water or feed her. And, as always, no answer came. She felt something touch her lips, something hard, and she recognized the texture of plastic as an uncapped bottle was pressed against her lips and tilted so she could drink. Candice gulped down the water, lots of it spilling down her chest, soaking her shirt. The water was coming too fast, and she coughed again. The bottle was removed.

"What do you want from me? Why are you keeping me here?" she asked again.

"I need you to shut up," the voice said.

"Why are you keeping me here?"

Silence.

"Tell me why?"

"You know why," the voice said after another a long pause, where she, for a minute, wondered if he had left her. It had happened before when she asked him questions. Instead of answering, he'd simply disappear.

Candice felt something else pressed against her lips. It was bread. She bit into it and chewed. She was starving, and this calmed her screaming stomach. While eating, she wondered what time it was and whether it was light or dark outside. She then wondered about Bryan and whether he was okay. Did he miss her like she missed him?

"Please," Candice tried. "You don't have to do this. You don't have to keep me here like this."

She hadn't seen his face when he had taken her. She had looked through the peephole before opening the door, but he had been wearing a baseball cap that was pulled down on his face. She felt certain she knew him, though; what she could see of him seemed familiar, and that was why she took off the chain and opened the door. That proved to be a big mistake. Now she was there, on the cold mattress on the floor, where she had woken up after he had knocked her out inside her apartment and apparently brought her somewhere else. She had thought that with all the screaming she did every time he pulled off the gag, that someone would come to her rescue, but so far, no one had. That told her that she probably wasn't in some condo in the city; she was somewhere else, somewhere where no one could hear her.

The bread disappeared, and more water was poured into her mouth. Candice drank, feeling like an animal. As the bottle was removed, the gag was pressed between her lips again, and her mouth covered with a cloth while she cried. Then she felt the barrel of the gun as it was placed against her forehead and pressed against her skin to make sure she could feel it.

"Now, you have some time to think about why I'm keeping you here. You need to think about what you have done. You only have yourself to blame for this, Candice. It's all on you."

Chapter 9

"YOU FAILED THE TEST? How is that even possible, Josie? You're so good at math?"

I was back at the station when Josie called, completely out of it, because she had gotten a zero on her math test online. Josie was excellent at math, so this was puzzling to me as well.

"I don't know, Dad. It's these stupid online tests; they're so…annoying. I hate this. I hate it. It's stupid anyway."

"You still have to do it if you want to pass this grade; you know this. But a zero, Josie? I don't believe you didn't even get one question right. What really happened?"

There was a long pause. I felt confused. It was so unlike Josie to fail a test, and not to get any questions right seemed almost impossible.

"Well…maybe I cheated on it, and my teacher found out," she finally said.

I dropped the pen in my hand. I stared into the almost empty police station. They had moved our desks apart, so we remained six feet from one another, and the few that were actually at work kept at a distance all day.

"You did what? You cheated? Josie!"

"Everyone does it. They have no way of finding out…usually."

"How did you cheat?"

"I found the answers online and then copied them into my test. It went faster that way. All the kids have been doing it since this online schooling started."

"And apparently, your teacher isn't as dumb as you thought she was," I said. "Well, there isn't much I can do about it. Hopefully, you have learned your lesson and will do your work yourself from now on."

"Can you tell Grandpa? Please?" Josie said. "I know he won't give me Animal Crossing when he finds out. He'll be all disappointed and all that."

"And why exactly can't you tell him yourself? You're in the house with him?" I asked. I stared at the screen in front of me, where I had searched for Bobby Kay Smith to find information about him. I hadn't had the time to look through much of it before Josie had called.

"I…well, it's embarrassing," she said.

That made me laugh even though this wasn't funny at all. "That's good. It will work as an important learning session. Go downstairs and tell him now, you hear me? Now, Josie."

She grumbled something, and we hung up. I returned to the screen, going through all the articles written about Bobby Kay Smith, or Bobby Kay as he usually went by.

He was a famous activist, known for arranging demonstrations, fighting for a higher level of equality in society. Often, he was known to use the slogan *Bobby Kay says it's not okay*. He was also known as sort of a hero around Miami, one that took it up with the big guys and fought for the little ones in society…the poor, the forgotten, the homeless. I had heard about him, but never really had that big an interest in him or his persona. Now, I was staring at his photo on my screen, trying to find out how to get ahold of him when my phone rang again.

It was Josie.

"What?"

Her voice was suddenly high and pitchy.

"It's Grandpa," she said. "He's on the couch downstairs. I think he has a fever. He's sweaty, and he's moaning. What do I do?"

My heart dropped as fear rushed through me in a huge wave. "Get away from him, Josie. Now! If he's sick, then you can't be near him. What might be like the flu to him could mean death to you. Get upstairs, now, Josie. I'm coming home!"

Chapter 10

THE SUN BAKED down on her head as she staggered down the empty streets, leaning on buildings on her way, walking from the taxi that had dropped her off as close to her home as they could get. Reese was sweating heavily but barely noticed. She couldn't believe what she saw, or rather didn't see.

Not a single soul was on the streets of Miami. No cars, no buses, no noise. It was so eerily quiet; she couldn't help feeling like the world had ended while she was out for four weeks. In her hand, she held her phone that she had in her pocket when she was taken to the hospital, according to the nurses. The battery was dead and hadn't been charged in weeks.

While resting herself against a building, she saw an ambulance parking in front of a condominium, and soon after, they rushed inside, wearing hazmat suits, pulling the stretcher. Reese stayed there for a few minutes, leaning against a wall. She breathed in the moist air and felt panic rise in her chest, fearing she was still sick, that she'd relapsed.

The nurses had told her she was the first to recover from this disease, so they had no idea if she was really over it or if it might come back. What recovery looked like, no one knew. She'd be the first to report on it. And they wanted her to call back in and tell them, so they knew what to tell other patients in the future. It filled Reese with panic that she didn't even know what her prospects were, what her future held. Would this mark her for the rest of her life? The virus had gotten in her lungs, and they had seen damage on the x-rays, they said, even some scarring, but would she recover from it completely, or would the scars remain there? No one knew. She was like a Guinea pig or a lab rat. That's how this felt.

Reese walked a few steps forward and regained some strength, at least enough to walk down her street, which had been blocked off. An officer in a Kevlar vest and helmet, looking like he might as well be off to war soon, drove up on her side and reached out his hand to stop her.

"Stop, ma'am. You shouldn't go in."

"But...I live here," Reese said. "Right down in that building over there."

"You live here?" he asked, puzzled.

Instinctively, Reese moved a step closer to better hear what he said since he had told her to stop when she was still like ten feet away from him. As she did this, he raised his weapon and pointed it at her from inside his patrol car.

"Stop right there, ma'am. Don't come any closer!"

Reese lifted her hands in the air and backed up, startled. She had never had the police point a weapon at her before.

"I'm sorry, sir. I just...I really want to go home."

She was almost crying now. This was all a bit much to take in for one day.

"The entire neighborhood has been closed off," he said. "For your own safety. This is where the virus outbreak started, right on this street. Hundreds of people have been hospitalized from this area, ma'am. You don't want to go in; trust me."

Reese bit her lip. Hundreds of people? Had *she* infected all those people?

Tears sprang to her eyes when thinking about this. Was she the reason for this outbreak? For all these people's deaths or misfortune?

"Ma'am?" the officer asked. "I really don't think you should go down there. It's for your own safety. The risk of being infected is very high in this area."

"But…" Reese said and looked at him sitting in his car, wearing a mask and gloves. She could see the fear painted in his eyes.

"Ma'am, you need to…"

"I have already had it."

The officer paused. He glared at her sideways.

"Excuse me?"

"I…I'm coming directly from the hospital, sir, and they said I already had the virus and recovered. The past two tests came back negative. I'm healed."

The officer stared at her. His hand on the weapon shook. "Ma'am, stay back, please. You could still be contagious. I haven't heard of anyone recovering as of yet…"

"But I did. I beat this thing."

She pulled out a letter that her doctor had given to her before she left. She hadn't read it, but he told her it said she was cured. It verified her as "Certified Recovered." The first one ever to be, he had proudly told her.

"I think it's safe for me to go back to my apartment," she said as she showed the document to the officer. He didn't take it in his hand, but read it from a distance, looking at her like he was certain she could kill him if she got close enough.

He shrugged, then said before he took off, "All right, ma'am. I guess you're safe here. Welcome home."

Chapter 11

I RODE like a madman through town on my Yamaha motorcycle, going way past the speed limit. It didn't make a difference since there wasn't a single car on the streets. Meanwhile, my heart hammered in my chest as I drove up in front of my townhouse. I killed the bike, then stormed inside and threw my helmet on the counter. I found my dad, lying on the couch in the darkness of the living room, then turned on the lights. My dad moaned, aggravated as the light hit his face. I could see the pearls of sweat on his forehead.

"Dad?"

I knelt next to him, still wearing my mask from work.

"Dad?"

Wearing gloves, I felt his wrist for a pulse. It was weak, and he didn't seem very responsive. He didn't say anything, and he didn't even open his eyes and look at me. He was moaning and tossing his head, and seemed to have chills all over his body. I found a blanket and covered him, then went to the kitchen and called our doctor.

"I fear my dad has gotten the virus," I said when he picked up.

Doctor Bird was a close family friend and had been our doctor since I was a child. He was getting older, but I preferred him over a younger version any day. He had lots of experience, and he knew us all so well. You couldn't put a price tag on that. Plus, I had his private number, and he'd always pick up when seeing it was me.

Doctor Bird paused on the other end. I could hear him breathing. He and my dad had been good friends and liked to go on fishing trips together.

"Oh, my word. Are you sure about this?" he asked. I could hear the distress in the tone of his voice. It sent a wave of fear through me.

"Tell me the symptoms," he said. "What are Bernard's symptoms?"

"He has a high fever."

"How high?"

"I haven't taken his temperature yet. But it's high. He's sweating and has chills. He's barely responsive. He's just lying on the couch, moaning. It scares me."

"Take his temperature as soon as you can, and then do so every three hours to keep track of it."

"Got it."

"Is he coughing?"

"No. At least not that I have heard yet."

"That's good. That's really good, Harry. It means it's not in his lungs. But a high fever at Bernard's age isn't a good sign. Make sure he doesn't lie on his back too much if he starts to cough. We don't want it to go into his lungs. Give him a fever reducer, Tylenol or Advil, and put a mask on him, so he won't spread the virus to the rest of you. Keep Josie away from him; do you hear me? This is important. You need to be careful around him, too, so you don't spread it to her. She's the vulnerable one here. No children have survived this so far. It can kill them within three days of showing the first symptoms. Is he in your home?"

"Yes. And he needs to stay here. He doesn't have anyone to take care of him," I said, fearing he'd tell me to take him back to his own house. I wouldn't be able to live with myself if I couldn't take care of my own dad. I couldn't just leave him alone at his house, sick with a deadly virus. That wasn't something I would ever agree to, and the doctor knew it.

"I understand. But keep him in a room alone and keep Josie from going in there. Disinfect everything, all door handles and surfaces, anything he could have touched today before he showed symptoms. And keep a close eye on both of them. If Josie starts to show symptoms, call me immediately. We'll get her to the hospital right away. With her heart condition, she's at high risk. Shoot, Hunter. I don't like to hear this. It scares me. Please, be careful."

"But...what about my dad? Isn't there anything you can do for him?" I asked. I was struggling to keep calm now. I felt so helpless. "Shouldn't he be getting to the hospital? Shouldn't he be getting some sort of treatment? Or at least be tested, so we know if this is the virus?"

Doctor Bird sighed. It wasn't a pleasant sound. It oozed deep frustration, and frankly, he wasn't making matters any better. He wasn't exactly calming me down this way.

"I'm sorry. This is the best we can do for now. If you're older than twenty-five, they won't take you in anymore. You can't even be tested. There aren't enough tests available. All the focus is on the young ones."

"But older people die from this, too, right?" I said, my voice rising in alarm and desperation. My dad meant the world to me. Was I just supposed to watch him get sick and maybe even die? Was there no help at all for him? Just because of his age? I couldn't believe this.

How did we get to this?

"I saw it on the news that a lot of older people are dying as well," I added. "My dad could die from this, and there's nothing we can do about it?"

"We need to think about our future," Doctor Bird said, his voice heavy. "There isn't enough room or ventilators at the hospitals. It's ordered from the top. They're our number one priority. The children are our future. We need to take care of them first. And right now, the hospitals are overwhelmed with patients fighting for their lives. That's why they had to make this decision. The rest of us will have to ride it out at home if we can. I'm sorry. I wish it didn't have to be this way, and you should be angry about it; I want you to be angry. But right now, there's nothing I can do. All you can do now is pray."

I hung up, annoyed at everything, including that saying. *All you can do now is pray*. Why did people always assume that was the last thing you should do? To me, it was my first response, and I had been praying all the way back here while driving on my bike. I prayed my dad would be okay, and I prayed that Josie would stay clear of this virus too. Now, I prayed that God would give me the strength to get through this and not let me succumb to fear. The temptation to let it overwhelm me was more than strong.

Chapter 12

I TOOK my dad's temperature, and that didn't exactly help my concerns. He had a hundred and two. This wasn't good for a man his age. I helped him drink water and got him to swallow a pill. While I did this, he opened his eyes and looked at me, but he didn't seem to really be there. His eyes were glassy and wet. He didn't seem to be looking directly at me, but at least I got to see him and was happy to see the pill slide down his throat. I covered him up and helped him get into the room in the back, where I knew he could stay away from Josie. I then washed down everything and disinfected all surfaces, then took a shower and washed myself thoroughly with soap and disinfected my hands again before I knocked on Josie's door and peeked inside, once again wearing my mask.

A set of very worried eyes looked back at me from the bed. I wanted to hug her but refrained from doing so in case I risked infecting her. We'd have to be very careful now, even though the odds of her not being infected were very low. She had spent the entire morning with my dad before he showed symptoms. They had been together for days since my dad moved in with us. They said you were contagious long before you showed symptoms, and my dad had been hanging out with us all weekend.

"How is he?" she asked, her voice sounding worried, even though she tried to hide it. "Will he be okay?"

I didn't know exactly how aware she was of the situation outside the four walls of our house. I tried to keep her protected from the worst stories. I didn't want her to be scared, but there was still the internet. It was very hard not to know what was going on, with all the stories on social media and in the news. I, for one, felt like I was constantly bombarded with information and horrifying stories from overwhelmed hospitals and doctors telling us how scared we should be, or press briefings with the president or our governor telling us all to please stay inside. It was hard not to know. Some people were watching the news non-stop, and it only filled them with fear and panic. For some, it was all they did all day since there really wasn't much else to do when you were on lockdown. Most people had lost their jobs or were furloughed. What else was there to do? I tried hard not to fall into that trap. I had made it a mantra to check the news and not watch it.

"He's sick, Josie," I said. I couldn't hide the truth from her. She deserved to know, but I was trying not to sound as alarmed as I felt.

"Is it the virus?" she asked, biting her nails.

"We don't know. But he has a high fever, and that is one of the symptoms."

"Will he need to go to the hospital?"

That was the hard one. I wasn't sure she'd be able to understand. I wasn't even sure I fully understood how you could refuse care for a man just because he was older.

"I spoke to Doctor Bird, and he told us to observe him, and then we'll see," I said. "But you need to stay in your room. I'll bring your food up here, so you can remain isolated from him. I put him in the back room, and you need to stay away from it; can you do that? I'll be the only one who goes in and out."

"But, Dad...what about you? You will risk getting infected too?" she said, her voice rising. "You could get sick, Dad."

"I know. That's why we need to keep our distance. You and me. So I won't infect you in case I do become contagious."

Her eyes grew big, and my heart dropped.

"So...we can't hug?"

I swallowed. This was as close to torture as I could get. There was nothing I loved more than holding my daughter in my arms. I couldn't believe this was what it had come to. I couldn't even kiss and hug my own child?

"I'm afraid not. At least not for now."

"Oh."

"I know," I said on the verge of tears. "It's terrible, but if it can save you from being infected, then it's a mild price to pay. I think we can do this, even if it is hard. I'll wear a mask even when walking around the house, and you should too. But try to stay in your room."

"I can't believe it," she said. "First, I'm not allowed to leave the house and see my friends; now, I can't go downstairs? I can't even leave my room? Can't we just clean everything?"

"I've disinfected as much as I could around the house, but I'm not sure it's enough. I fear it's not gonna be enough to protect you. Listen, it's not gonna be forever, just for a few days until we find out what is going on with Grandpa or until the areas he might have touched are clean. The virus can live up to two days on smooth surfaces, they say. It might seem excessive to keep you locked up in your room, but I feel this is what we need to do now. I need to feel safe, to feel like you're protected."

"What about when I need to use the bathroom?"

"Of course, you can go to the bathroom. But at least stay up here on this floor where Grandpa never comes anyway. It should be clean. I'll sleep in the living room to make sure I don't bring the virus up here as well. If you want something from downstairs, maybe you can just call for me? Or text me?"

Josie nodded. She seemed to be pondering this for a little while before finally accepting it.

"Okay. And what if I need a snack?"

"I'll bring it to you. I'll see if I can work from home for a few days. I'm sure my new boss, Major Walker, wouldn't want me to come in anyway and risk infecting everyone. I'll be here if you need me, okay? We'll get through this together with God's help. He is with us. He's helped us through tough times before, and He'll do it again. He'll never forsake us, remember?"

That seemed to make Josie calm down a little. She even got a little spark back in her eyes, and her lips curled into a smile.

"Okay, Dad. I think I'd like that snack now. Do we have any more of those Rice Krispy Treats?"

"I said you could get a snack, not poison yourself," I answered with a lifted eyebrow. "I'll bring you a banana."

Chapter 13

IT FELT good to get home. At least for the first few minutes. Reese sat on her couch in her living room. It was old and worn out, and the leather was falling off in patches. On the table in front of her, she had placed the pills the doctors had sent home with her, telling her *good luck*. Now she sat there in complete silence and was suddenly overwhelmed with deep sadness, one she didn't quite understand. It was like something was missing, yet she couldn't understand what. The place seemed so empty, more than usual. A wave of deep melancholy rushed through her, and she curled up in a fetal position, staring blankly into the room. She remembered being sick; she remembered not feeling well, but it was still a haze. She remembered walking some-where where there were a lot of people, and she remem-bered feeling dizzy and almost passing out. She remembered touching people's arms and them pushing her away like she was a nuisance, a drunk making a fool of herself. It kind of felt like she had been drunk—like there were these blanks she couldn't fill in. How had she gotten sick? The men at the hospital had wanted to know. But she didn't know. How could she tell them if she didn't remember? She had no idea who she had been in contact with or who could have infected her. But now, as she thought about it, she realized she could have caused all these people to get sick too. The crowd she had been in, the woman whose arm she had touched. Had she gotten sick too?

Reese shook her head and sat up straight. What was it about this place that made her so sad? She had lived alone for all her adult life, but suddenly, it felt like the condo was too empty, like it was impossible for her to be here alone.

Why? What had changed?

Reese got up and walked to the kitchen, then peeked inside the bedroom. The bed wasn't made. Reese never made her bed, so there was nothing strange about that. But there was something else. It felt like something was missing from the bed.

Not something.

Someone.

Reese walked inside and sat on the edge of it. She was so tired. The walk to her place from the taxi had exhausted her greatly. She had lost a lot of her muscles being bedridden for so long. It would take time to get them back. Plus, her lungs were damaged from the virus. The doctor had told her she would most likely feel tired and out of breath for quite some time, given what she had been through, how her body had fought for its life while they had her placed in an induced coma.

Thinking a little nap would do her good and might help her think more clearly, Reese put her head on the pillow and closed her eyes for a few seconds when she was certain she heard a baby cry. Gasping loudly, she opened her eyes and looked around her in the bed, searching for the source of the sound. But the sound was gone. She felt the covers and lifted them while breaking into a sweat, searching frantically for the baby.

Nothing.

It was just a dream, Reese. Don't let it get to you. You know it's all in your head. Stay in reality. Focus on what is real.

She put her head back down and closed her eyes, but as soon as she was about to doze off, she was certain she heard it again. She shot open her eyes and sat up straight, and now she couldn't escape the sound of the crying baby, even with her eyes open. It wasn't coming from the bed, but from inside her head—this persistent sound of a screaming and crying baby.

It was maddening.

Stop, please, just stop!

Reese held her hands to the sides of her head and wanted to scream to make it stop. She got up and staggered to the living room, leaning on furniture and walls. She stopped in the opening and stared at the floor. In front of her, on the wood, lay something that made her heart pound. Panting and agitated, Reese bent over and picked up a pink pacifier. She stared at the small item in her hand, her heart galloping in her chest as memories suddenly rushed in over her, overwhelming her so forcefully she thought she was going to die.

The crying intensified, and she could now see the baby's face in her mind as she closed her eyes and remembered the things she had forgotten, the things she didn't want to remember. Right then, she heard a noise coming from the other side of her door. Her eyes shot open, and she took a step closer, then stared at the white door, hands shaking.

The scratching noise was repeated, and soon the handle turned.

Chapter 14

RIGHT BEFORE MIDNIGHT had become my favorite time of day. That was when I'd stand out on the porch and wait for Jean to come home from a long workday. It was a big advantage that we lived right next door to one another. Otherwise, I wouldn't get to see her at all. She worked at the hospital, and the risk of her bringing the virus to my family and me was too great.

I sat on the patio swing, listening to the cicadas singing, waiting for her car to drive up the street. There was no other sound in the entire neighborhood, and I had to admit, I missed the noise. Usually—even at this hour—you could hear the highway or the train in the distance, or the endless sound of sirens blaring from downtown. But now there was suddenly nothing, and it filled me with deep sadness. I missed seeing life. I missed normalcy. Patrolling the streets during the day, seeing how empty our usually busy city was, made me sometimes feel a little panicky like the apocalypse had arrived. And every now and then, I wondered if it would ever go back to normal again. I know a lot of people felt the same way, and they missed the interaction with others. That's why you'd see them on social media singing from their balconies all over the world.

In our little neighborhood, I noticed people waved more at one another from the porches or the front yard while mowing the lawn. Every now and then, we'd have a rendezvous, each standing on our own porch, and we'd chat, yelling at one another just to get a little bit of human interaction that I don't think we understood how essential was to us until now. It really was like they said, you didn't know what you had till it was suddenly gone. Never had that saying been more fitting to a situation than now. I didn't know I'd miss my neighbors; I didn't know I'd miss the cars on my street, or seeing people walking the streets downtown. I didn't know I'd miss going shopping when I wanted to and not have it limited to once a week. I didn't know I'd one day miss being able to look into the eyes of my love or take her to dinner.

Just as I finished the thought, her car drove up the street, and I got up. Excited like a boy on prom night, I walked to the railing and watched her car as she drove past me. She waved out the window before she parked in her driveway. My heart threatened to jump out of my chest as she got out, and I could finally see her face. I could see the tracing of the mask she had worn all day etched into her skin. Her beautiful dark blue eyes lingered on me, and she got that look in them that made me so happy.

She's mine. She's all mine. And soon, I'll hold her in my arms again. Soon.

"Harry," she sighed and slammed the car door shut.

I swallowed the lump in my throat. How badly I wanted to run down and take her in my arms and just kiss her, pretending like this virus had never happened, like everything was back to normal and the rest had been nothing but a bad dream—a terrible, terrible nightmare.

"Jean," I sighed.

Seeing her made me so happy, I couldn't help but smile. I felt like I was about to explode. That's how badly I wanted to run to her.

Her eyes grew serious.

"How's your dad?"

I had texted her and told her he was sick. I didn't want to worry her, but I had to tell her. She adored my father, and he loved her just as much.

"He's sleeping," I said. "I took his temperature two hours ago, and it was the same, I am afraid. The Tylenol hasn't helped. I just hope he'll be able to break the fever during the night."

"And Josie?"

"Seems fine. At least for now. She's staying upstairs. I brought her dinner and placed it outside her door."

"That's gotta hurt," she said. She looked toward Josie's window. "No fun being a teenager locked up in your room. Is she going to be okay up there all alone?"

I nodded. "I think so. She's playing on her computer and doing these three-hour-long conference calls with her friends. I know she's scared and just doesn't want to show me. But right now, it's her health we've got to be worried about. I just find it hard to believe she hasn't been infected, you know? She was with my dad all weekend and this morning while I went to work. I'm watching over her like a darn hawk. It's like waiting for a bomb to go off, and you just don't know when."

Jean smiled compassionately. "There is a small possibility that she didn't get it. You gotta cling to that hope, Harry. Maybe she isn't infected."

"I'm afraid that I don't think that's very likely," I said with a deep exhale. "But here's to hoping, right?"

Jean tilted her head. "How are you coping, Harry? It's gotta be tough. It's a lot right now for you."

I shook my head with a scoff. "You're unbelievable, do you know that? Here you are, coming home from the front lines of the war. You've been saving people, taking care of them all day, watching people—some of them children— die right in front of you, and still you have the energy and compassion to ask me how I am holding up."

She shrugged. "What can I say? It's in my blood to take care of people. I can't help myself."

"How was today?" I asked. "At the hospital?"

Jean's eyes grew weary, and I regretted asking.

"Tomorrow will be better."

My heart sank. This was her way of saying it had been awful and that tomorrow could only be better.

"You're amazing," I said and smiled gently. I was so in love with this woman at this moment; it seemed impossible.

"We all gotta do what we can," she said. "And this is what I am good at."

"Do you have time for a glass?" I asked.

Since the lockdown started, every night when she came home, we'd sit on each of our porches and have a glass of wine together, yet apart, while catching up on our day. It was the highlight of my entire day, and I especially needed it tonight.

Jean smiled back gently, completely melting away my heart.

"I thought you'd never ask."

Chapter 15

I CALLED the major the next morning and told him that my dad had gotten sick. He took it very seriously, and, according to protocol, I was told to stay home. We started contact tracing just in case it was the Florida Flu that my dad had contracted, and my partner, Propper, was sent home too. I knew he would be very upset about that, but those were the rules. I continued working on the case of the missing woman from home and read more about her brother, Bobby Kay, the famous activist and founder of the group OUTRAGED. Bobby Kay was a DJ and poet from Miami. His group was initially known as a running club, dedicated to *changing and empowering the next generation*. The group mostly consisted of artists, activists, and influencers that used the platforms they had, primarily online, to speak about issues that were important to them. The environment was a big issue for most, but also social issues like women's rights, and the rights of the LGBT community and civil rights. They were known to arrange protest runs in and around Miami. But they were most active in the online community, where they could connect to a lot of viewers—especially young people. They had tons of followers on their social media accounts and YouTube.

Naturally, a guy like him didn't leave his phone number out anywhere. So, I contacted Bobby Kay through his Facebook page. I wrote him a private message, leaving my number, telling him to call me, saying that I needed to talk to him about his sister, stressing it was important.

My dad stayed in the room in the back, but I could hear his moans all the way in the living room. His breathing had become faster and shallower. His fever was the same this morning, and he hadn't eaten in almost twenty-four hours now. He barely drank any water, and that had me worried. I was scared he'd dehydrate.

Josie was still showing no symptoms. I, for one, had barely slept all night since I had been awake, worrying that she was in her room, sick, unable to tell me. But as I knocked on her door this morning and peeked inside, I found her lying in bed with her computer in her lap. She smiled back at me before she ordered pancakes for breakfast.

Naturally, I made her all the pancakes she could eat and even put small chocolate chips in them to make them extra delicious. I also cut up a bowl of fruit for her, mostly to ease my sense of guilt for giving her an unhealthy breakfast. She was happy with both and ate it all, though. At least the fruit gave her some vitamins for her body to build up her immune system. Or at least that's what I told myself when I felt panic rise in my chest. It was hard not to let the fear overpower me. I fought a tough fight to keep the images of her in the hospital, intubated and fighting for her life, at bay. Still, I lost the struggle from time to time, and I had a small panic attack in the kitchen, thinking about her dying in there and me not even being able to visit or say goodbye.

The thought was unbearable.

After writing the message for Bobby Kay, I finished up a report from two weeks ago on another case that I had neglected. I went through my emails, then accidentally went on Facebook and scrolled through my newsfeed.

I should never have done that. All I saw were images of nurses in hazmat suits telling us how awful it was at the hospitals or doctors telling us to please stay home. For some reason—I don't know why—I read the story of some celebrity who had the virus and wrote about it for her fans, telling people this was *no joke* and the worst thing she'd ever experienced.

This is no flu; please, stay home.

She also said her son now had it and that he was just admitted to the part of the hospital where no one returned from; no one recovered—where body bags were piling up in the hallways.

People are dying from this. Kids are dying. Hold your children tight tonight; I might never hold my boy again.

I felt my heart rate going up, reading this and hurried past it without reading it to the end. Next, I saw videos of people's dogs doing tricks and scrolled past tons of memes and gifs about how people now drank at ten a.m. because they had nothing better to do, and then saw posts from an old friend of mine who was showing pictures of the slow-roasted turkey she was making for dinner. I ended my scrolling when a political post from a friend turned ugly, and I found myself reading the comments from all the trolls, who seemed to believe that this virus had emerged from the cell phone towers and that it was the government's way of trying to control us all. Realizing this was doing me no good, I shut the phone off and put it on the table. I exhaled, trying to shake all these emotions and was about to grab myself some iced tea when there was a sound outside my door. A second later, a knock followed. Puzzled at who could be at my door, I walked over and opened it.

The eyes meeting me on the other side almost made me start to cry.

Chapter 16

"REESE?"

My sister's big blue eyes stared up at me. She was tall for a woman, six feet tall, but with my six-foot-eight, I still towered above her, even though she was my older sister.

I looked down at her, my heart beating fast, and I realized I was barely able to breathe. I hadn't seen her in about a year, maybe even more. It felt like forever. I had been so worried about her.

"What are you…how…?" I stuttered.

"Can I come in?"

I looked at her when reality sank in. I took a step backward, remembering. "I thought you were in the ICU? They called dad from the hospital and told him you'd been admitted with a strange virus they didn't know what was, and then told him we couldn't visit. You were patient zero, we were later told, the first one to have it. We were so worried and didn't think you'd make it."

"But I did," she said, sending me a weak smile. She threw out her arms. She had a weak and exhausted look to her eyes and could only stand for a few seconds without holding onto the door frame. "Look. I'm well now. They said I had recovered, then sent me home."

I stared at her, scrutinizing her. My sister had been mentally ill since we were teenagers, struggling with her anxieties ever since she was raped. She was later diagnosed with schizophrenia and had a hard time keeping a job or even living a normal life. She struggled with paranoid delusions and sometimes hallucinations. I never knew if I could trust what she told me. She lived in a world of her own for the most part. Her medicine could usually keep it at bay, but not always.

"Are you sure about that?" I asked. "I mean, I can see that you're better; you're here, standing up—well, almost. But are you sure you're not still contagious?"

Reese swallowed. Her big eyes lingered on my face. I loved her so much, and I was relieved to see her alive. I wanted to hug her, but I couldn't.

"The doctor said I was well and not contagious anymore," she said. "You can see it in this letter he gave me."

She held up a letter in which a doctor from Jackson Memorial Hospital wrote that Reese was "Certified Recovered."

"It doesn't say you're not contagious," I said, concerned. I wanted terribly to let her inside my house, but I had to think about Josie. "I read that they don't know if you can still infect others. They know so little about this new virus."

"I tested negative twice," she said, shaking her head. "I don't have it anymore."

I smiled gently—how I had missed my dear sister. I was used to her disappearing out of my life for weeks, maybe even months at a time, but never this long. When I heard she had been hospitalized, I had been so certain she wouldn't make it, but here she was, standing right in front of me. It was hard to believe.

"How are you feeling?" I asked.

"I'm okay, I guess. I'm tired and out of breath from walking. I feel like I'm eighty years old, heh. But other than that…"

"What's that?" I asked suddenly when looking at her arm. A red patch was soaking her shirt. "Are you bleeding?"

She got a strained look on her face, then nodded.

"I…I didn't know where else to go."

I felt my heart rate go up. "That's a lot of blood, Reese; come inside and let's take a look at it."

Chapter 17

I HELPED her take her shirt off, carefully, then looked at her arm. She had a long cut running up her upper arm. It was deep, but it had stopped bleeding. I cleaned it and bandaged it while remembering the many times she took care of me when we were children. She had been the strong one back then. She had taken care of me. It wasn't until she reached seventeen that things began to go south for her. Since then, her life had been a struggle, one I didn't believe she deserved at all. I had prayed for God to set her free for as long as I could remember.

"There," I said, looking at the bandaged arm. I wasn't much of a paramedic, but I had gotten some training and knew how to do simple things. "You're as good as new. Almost."

Reese smiled with a small sigh. I could tell she was troubled about something, and she was waiting for the right moment to tell me.

"So, are you going to tell me what happened?" I asked and nodded at the bandaged area. "To your arm?"

She swallowed, and her upper lip vibrated slightly like it used to do when we were children, and she was scared.

"What's going on, Reese?" I asked. "Please, tell me."

Her shoulders came down. "I think someone is trying to kill me, Harry."

I wrinkled my eyebrows. I had heard her say stuff like this so many times before and knew to be cautious what I believed.

"What do you mean?"

"When I got back from the hospital, I was in my apartment, when...there was someone there, Harry, the handle...it was moving and then I...I...managed to get to the fire escape. I think...I think...no, I know someone came into my apartment and was after me. I saw a shadow rush across the room from outside on the fire escape. I hid there until he was gone."

"Do you have any idea who it might be?" I asked.

She shook her head.

"Could it maybe have been someone you knew?"

"I don't know."

"Was the door locked?"

She nodded. "Yes. I think so."

"So, how did he come in? Did he have a key?" I asked.

"He kicked it open," she said. "I heard it break as I crawled across the living room toward the fire escape."

I bit the side of my cheek, wondering about this story. My sister had had her share of shady boyfriends. It wouldn't be the first time she was scared of one of them.

"And the arm? How did you get the deep cut?"

She looked up at me like she didn't know what I was talking about. Then she looked down at her arm again and seemed to remember suddenly.

"Oh, yes. I...I...I'm not sure, Harry. I think I fell. Yes, that was it. I fell, and there was a spike in the fire escape...

if only I could get my mind to stop spinning." She tapped herself with a fist on the forehead. "I can't seem to remember much about anything these days, Harry. You know how I get."

"Are you off your meds?"

She looked away.

"Reese? Did you go off your meds again?"

She nodded vaguely.

"How long? How long have you been off?"

I was fighting to keep calm. She knew how important those meds were and what would happen if she got off them. How could she be so stupid?

"I had to go off, Harry," she said.

I sighed. *Here we go again*, I thought. *Here comes the usual story of how the meds make her brain foggy, how she feels like she's someone else, and she can't think clearly.*

Reese was rubbing her face excessively. "I don't remember, Harry, but it's been a long time. I didn't realize it until I got back to the apartment, but now I remember something. I think I got off the meds because I had to."

"You had to? What is that nonsense? You have to stay on them. There is no reason why you shouldn't take them at all."

"But there is, Harry. Don't you see?"

"I really don't, no. You're starting to ramble. You're making no sense, Reese."

She was biting her lip as she looked me in the eyes. "They told me I had to get off my meds. The doctors did."

"And why would any doctor tell you to go off your meds?" I asked, exhaling tiredly. This wasn't exactly what I needed right now.

She grasped my arm, squeezing it hard. "For the baby. They told me that I couldn't have a baby while still on my meds. I risked harming it. That's why they wanted to remove it, to kill it, but I didn't let them. Instead, I stopped taking the pills. For the baby's sake. I didn't remember this till I found the pacifier at my apartment; look."

Reese reached into her pocket and pulled out a pink pacifier. "I think it was a girl, but I am not completely sure."

Chapter 18

I DIDN'T BELIEVE my own ears. I stared at my sister, feeling so confused.

"You had a baby, Reese? But how is that possible?"

She shook her head. "I don't know. You know how it is with my memory, but I do remember being pregnant; I remember my growing stomach, and I remember giving birth. I keep seeing her when I close my eyes, and I can hear her too. My sweet baby girl. She reminded me of you when you were just a baby—all wrinkled and red like a small prune."

I swallowed, trying to contain all this new information. "So, you're telling me you had a baby against the doctor's recommendations?"

"A baby girl, yes. I'm pretty sure. Abby. I called her Abby…I think. I always liked that name, so I guess I would pick that for her."

"Who is the father? Do you even know?"

She gave me a guilty look. Usually, the guys my sister dated never stayed for more than a few weeks at a time. I guessed he was long gone.

She shook her head. "I don't remember."

"And where is the baby now?"

Her eyes filled. "That's what I don't know."

"You don't know? How can you not know this?"

"I didn't even remember having her until I got back, Harry. I was in a coma for four weeks. I have no idea what happened before that. I remember someone crying, and I remember my baby girl lying in bed with me, but that's all."

"So, she's just...gone?" I asked, sounding a little angrier than I wanted to. "And you don't know where she is?"

My sister bit her lip again and nodded. "I'm sorry. I am so, so sorry. I fear that...I was sick, you know? They say I fainted in a supermarket. They took me to the hospital, where they realized something was very wrong. I could barely breathe, and they had to intubate me. That's when they put me in an induced coma."

"And by then, you had already infected a lot of people, including nurses and doctors. They didn't know you were carrying a new virus no one had ever seen before, that no one was immune to. And by the end of the week, it had spread to the entire state, And here we are, almost four weeks later, and the entire world has closed down. Wow. Do you have any idea how you got the virus?"

She shook her head again. "No. They asked me all these questions at the hospital too, but I couldn't answer them, Harry. You know how my memory is. I can't distinguish between what is in my head and what isn't. I thought the baby was just something I had made up until I found the pacifier and suddenly remembered her. Oh, God, what if she died? What if I infected her with the virus, and then she died? I keep hearing her crying; I'm so scared, Harry. What could have happened to her?"

I exhaled and leaned back, quite baffled. Here I thought things had gotten as bad as they possibly could. But I guess not.

"I don't know, Reese. I didn't even know you had a child. I can't believe you had a baby, and you didn't even tell Dad or me."

"I meant to tell you. I did. You must believe me, but things went so fast and I couldn't…I was afraid you'd tell me to get rid of it like the doctors did because I couldn't. I wanted this child; I wanted her more than anything. She was the one thing right with me…that I ever did right. After I had given birth, I wanted to come to visit and show her to you, that was my plan, but then I don't know what happened. I can't seem to separate the days. I thought I… but then… Oh, Harry, I don't know what happened or how it all happened. I am so confused. I need your help, Harry. Today, someone came for me. I know they did. They came into my apartment and wanted to kill me, and I am so scared. Please, Harry, please, tell me you'll help me."

I stared at her, then reached out and pulled her into a deep hug, forgetting all the rules of social distancing and fear of her infecting me. Her skinny body was shaking in my arms as I held her tight and kissed the top of her head while wondering how much of this story I could actually believe was true. How much of this story was just her disease talking or the voices in her head?

"Of course, I'll help you, Reese," I said, rocking her back and forth the same way she used to do with me when I was crying as a child.

"Of course, I will."

Chapter 19

SHE HEARD FOOTSTEPS APPROACHING. Frantically, Candice tried to wrench her hands free, but she couldn't. Pain shot through her arms as the strips bit into her skin. The grating sound of a door being opened followed. Candice held her breath behind the gag. She had recognized her captor's voice, but she couldn't place it. He tried to change it when he spoke to her, making it deeper, so she wouldn't recognize it, but there was something very familiar about it, and it scared her. This was no random kidnapping. This was planned.

Think about what you have done, he had said. Naturally, it was all she could think about when he left her alone.

Why had this guy targeted her? Did it have to do with her work?

The door slammed shut behind her captor, and she knew she was no longer alone. Her heart rate quickened as she heard the footsteps approach. She felt how she was panting, agitated and whimpering, wondering what would be next for her. Images of rape kept nagging at her constantly, especially in the beginning. Was that why he had taken her? To have his way with her?

No. You can't let fear get the better of you. You must remain calm and collected. Only in that way can you survive.

A hand touched her cheek, and she winced. The hand lingered on her cheek for a few seconds, and Candice had to focus on calming herself, so didn't panic run off with her. She felt herself hyperventilating and almost choking behind the gag.

"Don't be scared," he whispered.

She could hear his breathing close to her ear. What was it about that voice that was so familiar? Was it someone she knew well? A friend or a co-worker? No, that couldn't be it. It somehow felt further away, distant. Could he be someone she might have met in a bar on one of her nights out? Someone she had rejected? A former blind date come back for more? Come back for what he believed was his, what he was entitled to?

The hand was removed, and she felt him walk away. He was still in the room; she was certain of it. She hadn't heard the door open and close again, and now she could hear something else. It sounded like a zipper being opened on a backpack or a suitcase, maybe. Had he brought something? Toys for his sex games? Instruments for torturing her?

The thought made her gasp behind the gag, and she fought to breathe properly to calm her beating heart.

What was her kidnapper's plan? Was it going to be painful?

Please, God, no. Please.

Candice slid down onto the mattress below her, her torso shaking in fear. As she laid her head down, her blindfold slid up slightly, just enough for a little light to enter. Almost blinded by it, she closed her eyes briefly, startled. After a few seconds, while her kidnapper was busy with his bag, pulling things out, she managed to peek out just enough to see him. She couldn't see his face since he had his back turned to her and was wearing a surgical mask like most people were these days when going outside like the governor had urged them to.

She couldn't see his face or see him properly, but she could see what he was pulling out of his backpack, and the sight made her just about lose it.

Candice didn't know much about explosives, but she did know that's what she was looking at. Her heart almost stopped as she worried this guy might make a mistake and blow them both up, but his hands moved with what seemed like expertise and experience. Praying under her breath, she watched as he worked with great caution, then attached a wire to the backpack holding the explosives and trailed it from the backpack to the door. Then he left her, closing the door carefully behind him.

Again, Candice was no expert, but it didn't take a genius to see that if anyone tried to come through that door, the bomb would be triggered. Realizing this, she lay completely still, listening, hearing nothing but the heavy beating of her frightful heart.

Chapter 20

HARRY HAD GIVEN her the couch and was sleeping on the floor himself. Reese laid awake most of the night, staring into the ceiling or looking at her handsome little brother, snoring away next to her.

Always the gentleman.

He had found a new girlfriend, he had told her, and she had gotten his entire story of the past year, during which he had lost his wife. She was now in a witness protection program and had changed her identity and everything. It was quite the story, and Reese felt sad that her brother had to go through this. But she was happy he had found Jean. She seemed like a nice girl, and Harry looked so in love when seeing her. Reese had said hello to her, standing on the porch before they went to bed when Harry went out to see her as she returned from working at the hospital. Reese had gone back inside to let them talk, and Harry had stayed out there for at least an hour, while Reese watched TV in his living room, trying not to listen in on their conversation.

She had sat with their dad for a little while, holding his

hand while he slept. He was still burning up and had started to cough. Reese was worried about him. She knew what he was going through. She didn't exactly remember much from when she began to get symptoms, but she did remember that it didn't feel good. For her, it had started with a fever just like their dad, and then a burning sensation in her lungs and a deep cough had followed. She didn't recall exactly when it began, but it was bad once it started. She coughed and coughed all night long and had to sit upright to sleep. It had felt like she would suffocate.

Abby? Where was the baby at this point?

Reese didn't remember her from when she was sick, but how could that be? Had she contracted the virus and died? Had she buried her somewhere?

Reese couldn't stand the thought of not knowing. It was eating at her. She feared the baby was lying somewhere, crying for her mother. She kept hearing her cries as she closed her eyes, and it felt like torture.

When realizing she wasn't going to get any sleep, Reese got up from the couch and walked to the kitchen. She found some iced tea in the fridge and poured herself a glass. She was still out of breath from even the smallest of efforts, and she got dizzy from standing up, then sat in a chair at the dining table. The sound of Harry's snoring filled the room and made her calm.

No one made her calm like Harry.

Reese felt sadness overwhelm her when thinking about the many people filling the hospitals right now all over the world. She couldn't help feeling like it was all her fault— like she was to blame for their misfortune. Not to mention the millions of people that would be unemployed after this because of the economy and a possible recession. That's what they had said on TV. Reese didn't know much about that, but she had heard the experts talking about it, and it saddened her deeply. So many of the people in the super-market where she had fainted had become sick afterward. So many doctors and nurses who had treated her, who didn't know what they were dealing with—how many more had she infected? She had been contagious for days before she fainted in that supermarket, the doctor had told her. Not that they knew for sure, but that was their theory. Perhaps it could have been more. In all that time, she had been out and about in society. Reese often rode the bus or the train that also went to the airport. She worked at a CVS where many people came and went. Seven of her coworkers were in the hospital now; Harry had told her—including her boss. One of the infected clients who had frequented the CVS where she worked was also a teacher at a local high school and had spread it to the students. One particular school had more than four hundred kids in the hospital. Many of them had died.

How am I supposed to live with myself after this? How am I supposed to continue, knowing I have caused this, that I was the one infecting them all? I caused this Armageddon. I caused it all!

Reese sniffled and drank her iced tea. Then she folded her hands and did something she hadn't done in years. Being a pastor's daughter, she had been quick to reject God and everything her dad stood for as a teenager, espe-cially after the rape. She had thought God had left her, and she turned her back on him. How could she not when she had prayed for His help while she was being raped, and He had stayed silent? How could she believe He wanted what was best for her? How could she believe He was for her when He let this happen? When He didn't stop it? She hadn't prayed for his help since, but she was doing that now. It was time to stop running.

"God, if you still remember me," she whispered into the darkness of the room, while tears spilled onto her cheeks. "I need your help. I'll do anything you tell me to. I am in so much pain, and I don't know how to make things right again. Help me find my baby. Help me. Please."

Reese sat like that for a few minutes, realizing this was the clearest she had been able to think since she was let out of the hospital. She slowly remembered things from the time before. Harry had taken her to the drive-thru pharmacy and made sure she got new meds, and she already felt better than she had in a very long time. The voices were still there, but she was less anxious, and the paranoia seemed to have settled slightly too. Her mind was still racing with images and thoughts that she didn't know where they came from or if they were true or not, but it was definitely an improvement.

Reese finished her iced tea, then rose to put the glass in the dishwasher when she thought she heard a sound coming from behind her. Gasping, she turned around and saw someone, a figure standing by the window outside.

Reese stopped and stared at the figure, heart racing in her chest.

Was he real? Or was he just in her mind?

There was no way for her to tell.

Reese closed her eyes for a few seconds, then opened them again, and the figure was gone. She sighed, relieved. It was just her imagination, her paranoia. It was nothing.

She closed the dishwasher, then walked to the living room, where Harry was still snoring. She laughed quietly at him, then sat on the couch and stared at her baby brother for a few seconds, finally feeling a little tired, hopefully enough to be able to go to sleep.

Reese laid down, pulled the blanket over her shoulders, and closed her eyes. As she did, she saw Abby again. This time, she was lying on a blanket on the floor while Reese was changing her diaper and tickling her stomach. Abby was cooing, and then she pulled her lips into a small smile.

Her first smile.

Reese's heart skipped a beat, and she opened her eyes with a gasp, smiling from ear to ear when remembering this, realizing it was no dream; it was real. She remembered it vividly.

As she opened her eyes, she looked right into the face of a dark shadow towering above her. She didn't see it, but she felt the blade of the knife as it was pressed against the skin on her throat.

Chapter 21

I WAS DREAMING ABOUT JEAN, a strange dream where she was far away from me, and I couldn't get to her. She was sick and couldn't breathe, and I could hear her calling my name, but I couldn't find her. I was pulled out of the dream with a loud gasp when something woke me.

It took me a second or two to realize what was happening. At first, I couldn't believe what I was looking at, it was so surreal, but once I got my sight back, I realized Reese was in trouble.

There was a person bent over her, and she was struggling.

I shot up, then rose to my feet in the same swift movement and sprang for him, knocking him sideways into the wall behind the couch. The knife was still in his hand, and he swung it at me, cutting me on the shoulder. I fell back and placed a hand on the wound, while Reese screamed and kicked. She tried to escape, but the person grabbed her and stabbed the knife at her. Reese moved just in time, and the knife went into the couch instead and ripped a huge tear in the fabric. A second later, I was back on my feet. I swung my fist and hit him on the jaw so hard he flew back and crashed into my lamp. He scrambled to his feet, then ran for the door. I jolted after him and was inches from grabbing his collar, but missed. He unlocked the front door, then stormed outside. By the time I was on the porch, he was running down the street and disappeared between the houses.

I stood there, panting and wiping sweat from my face when Reese came up behind me.

"Who was that?" I asked. "Did you know him?"

She shook her head. "I...I don't know."

"Did you see his face?"

She shook her head and turned around.

"Reese?" I grabbed her by the shoulder and turned her to force her to look at me. "You know who he is, don't you?"

She looked up at me, then shook her head. "I don't know who he is."

"But you did recognize him, didn't you?"

"Maybe. I...I don't know, Harry." She exhaled, frustrated, and sat on the patio swing. She was hitting her head with her fists. "I just can't...I don't know. I know him, yes. At least I think so. I think I recognized the eyes, but I could barely see them properly with the sparse light in the living room. It was pretty dark. And I don't know where I should know him from."

"But maybe he is someone you met while you were off your meds," I said.

"If it is the same guy, then I have seen him in my mind. In images," she said. "I thought it was just a dream or one of my paranoid hallucinations, you know? I've had so many of them lately. It's hard for me to tell the difference."

I pulled her into a hug, calming myself and my pounding heart.

"Of course. I know it's hard for you."

"I told you that someone was trying to kill me," she said, her body shaking in my arms. "I'm so scared."

"Of course, you are. We need to get you somewhere safe. I know just the place."

Chapter 22

"HOW WILL I know that she won't infect me?"

Al was wearing a surgical mask, plastic gloves, and glasses when she opened the door after unlocking the many locks on the other side.

"I told you this on the phone, Al," I said. "She's recovered. If there's anyone it's safe to be around right now, it's her."

Al gave Reese a suspicious look, then glared at me again. "I'm not happy about this."

"I don't think any of us are happy right now," I said. "She has nowhere else to go. Someone attacked her in her own apartment and tried to kill her. The same person tried to kill her in my house last night too. We need your help. Please, Al."

Al pulled aside with a reluctant grunt and let us in. She closed the door behind us and locked it safely. Her dining room table was topped with weapons—guns and even an AK47. I turned to face her.

"What's going on here?"

"Just preparing," she said.

"For what? Guerilla war?"

Al glared at me from above the rim of the glasses. "You don't know what I know."

"What do you mean?" I asked. "Tell me; what's going on?"

She walked to her desk. It had seven monitors on it, all showing surveillance cameras from all over the world, some even from people's homes. Al "The Plague" Alvita, was a former CIA hacker, but what she did for a living now, I didn't know. I had a few ideas and believed she might be working for private companies, but I tried not to think about it.

"There's been a lot of chatter; let's just leave it at that, okay?" she said.

"A lot of chatter?" I asked, definitely not ready to leave this alone.

"Online, on the underground web fora," she said. "On the dark web, all the shady places, they're talking about this virus. Even government officials are talking. Something is going on, and I, for one, am keeping myself ready."

I shook my head. "Are we talking a state coup here or what? I thought it was just a virus?"

"There is no such thing as just a virus, Hunter. Don't be naïve. Look what it has done to us, to the entire world? Has any other virus ever done this to us? Look at how fast it spread? In just a few days, four weeks in total, it reached the entire world? How's that even possible? No other virus has ever done that. Researchers say the virus stems from snakes. But how does a snake virus suddenly jump to humans when it hasn't done that before?"

"It mutated?" I said with a shrug.

"The thing is, normally, the snake virus can't penetrate humans. It lacks a protein, what the experts call the S-protein. It's simply impossible for it to harm us. But if you add this lacking protein to a virus, it suddenly becomes deadly to humans. It becomes transmittable to humans. The question is, how did the virus suddenly acquire this extra protein in its DNA?"

"What are you trying to say?" I asked. Reese sat down on the couch. She was tired and confused. I didn't like the look on her face. She seemed so lost.

"It was created," Al said. "This virus was manufactured to attack us. That's what they're all saying in the chats, including all the medical and virology experts who won't dare to stand up and tell the world what they know because they have no proof, yet they all agree. This virus was created in a lab, then released on us."

I stared down at the small woman in front of me. Al tended to be paranoid due to the work she used to do and the things she had seen. She knew stuff I was sure I didn't want even to know was going on, especially when seeing what it did to her. She lived a lonely life, afraid to leave her house, trusting no one, and I didn't want that life. Even if it meant me living in complete oblivion to what was really going on in the world, I believed ignorance could sometimes be bliss.

But even though I had heard some crazy talk from her over the years, I had never heard her talk like this before.

"What are you saying?" I asked. "Who would do something like that?"

She shrugged and sat by her screens, then tapped on her keyboard. "The government, a private company who already owns the vaccine, who knows? But I am not letting them get away with it, no matter who is behind this. I intend to find out who they are." Al turned and smiled at Reese, who seemed even more confused than ever.

"And having patient zero here might actually prove to be a blessing in disguise."

Chapter 23

I LEFT them for a few hours to go home and take care of my family. My dad's cough had gotten hollower, and now he was experiencing shortness of breath as well. I made a tray of food for Josie, then walked upstairs with it and placed it outside the door and knocked. I took a few steps back to keep my distance from her when she opened the door. Then I called her name.

"Josie? Food is here."

It took a few seconds before the door handle turned, and she peeked out. My heart skipped a beat when seeing her as I realized how terribly I missed her, missed being close to my own daughter. She smiled when seeing me.

"How are you feeling?" I asked, worried about the answer. Was she a little pale? Were her eyes weary?

"I'm okay; I guess," she said with a small shrug.

"No fever? Any body aches?"

She shook her head. "I don't think so. I've been very tired all day yesterday and this morning."

My heart dropped. Fatigue was one of the first symptoms. This wasn't good. Had she become symptomatic?

Would she get a fever soon and then start to cough? I forced a smile, trying not to show her how scared I was. Then, something hit me.

"Have you been up all night, maybe? Getting to bed a little too late, playing computer games?"

That made her smile. "Maybe. Kinda."

I sighed with relief. There was an explanation. The fact that she was feeling tired didn't have to mean she had been infected. Maybe she was just being a teenager. After all, there was nothing unusual about a teenager experiencing fatigue. Maybe, just maybe, she was still all right.

"Try to get to bed at a decent time tonight, will you?" I asked. "It also helps your immune system, and we're trying to keep you healthy here."

She sighed. "I know. It's just so boring, Dad. I stay in my room all day and have nothing to do. I have online friends across the globe that I play with, and they're awake at night when I am supposed to sleep."

"I know, sweetie. I know. You can't change your rhythm to be awake all night and sleep all day. That's not healthy. I know it's no fun right now. Believe me; I don't find it particularly amusing either. It's tough being apart and being locked in like this. But it's necessary to keep you safe."

"You keep saying that. But I'm fine. How's Grandpa?" she asked, her eyes worried. "Is he better?"

I looked down, then shook my head. "I am afraid he's getting worse. But I'm sure he'll get better soon. I don't want you to worry, you hear me?"

"Well, I do," she said, tears welling up. "It's pretty hard not to."

I took a deep breath and exhaled. I knew what she meant. I was extremely worried too.

"I'm sure he'll be fine."

"You don't sound very convincing," she said with a scoff. "I read yesterday that people over the age of sixty are more likely to die from this virus because the hospitals aren't taking them in anymore. How can they do that? They're people too? Plus, they're old, and they need care more than younger people."

"They're thinking about the kids," I said. "This virus is tough on the younger generation, and a lot have already died from it. The hospitals have reached their capacity. They simply don't have room for them."

"But aren't old people human too?"

That was a hard one. I couldn't really argue against that. I wondered how we were going to look back at this afterward. At the decisions that were being made, how much we were going to regret. Then I wondered about Al and what she had told me. No one knew how this virus had originated. And up until now, no one had really focused on it since everything had happened so fast, and focus had remained only on the survival of the population and especially the children. But for the first time, I was thinking about just that while watching my daughter take in her tray and send me a feeble smile. I wondered who was responsible for this mess that right now seemed like it was about to destroy so incredibly many lives.

Chapter 24

WHEN I RETURNED to Al's place, they were both sitting at her screens, the chairs placed with space between them. I sensed that Al was slowly accepting that Reese wasn't contagious anymore, but still taking precautions.

"We've been busy," she said as she let me in and returned to her seat. I stood behind her, looking over her shoulder, not getting too close. After all, I had a sick dad at home, even if I did take all the precautions in the world and made sure I was completely clean when leaving the house, even changing my clothes and wearing both gloves and a mask, the risk of me infecting Al was still pretty big, and we both knew it.

I was taking my own temperature three times a day to make sure that if I had the least bit of an elevation, I could stay home. So far, I was fine, and I felt good too, not counting the nagging worry in the pit of my stomach that had become my steady companion lately.

"Yeah? You found anything?"

Al tapped on her keyboard and pulled up a video on the screen in front of her.

"We have been tracing your sister's whereabouts using facial recognition software," Al said. "This is the video from the supermarket downtown, where she fainted in the middle of a crowd."

Al started the clip, and I saw Reese walking around the supermarket. She wasn't picking up many groceries; she was mostly just pushing her cart around, walking down one aisle, then stopping to lean on the shelves before continuing. It was obvious in the clip that she was sick and fighting to make it through. She seemed confused, walking down one aisle, then another like she didn't know what she had entered the store to get. Finally, she grabbed a gallon of milk, then walked to the bread section, where she stood for a little while, leaning on her cart before she seemed to decide to leave. She pushed the cart down the aisle toward the registers, then got in line to pay for the milk and bread. While waiting, people were standing very close to her, almost crowding her, and she was leaning onto the cart, barely keeping upright. As it was almost her turn, her legs suddenly gave way beneath her, and she slid to the floor. A huge crowd surrounded her immediately. Some came running to help, getting close to her, bending down over her. Someone knelt next to her, then put her face close to Reese's and felt for a pulse. Next, she performed CPR, giving Reese mouth to mouth.

Al paused the video. "This woman saved Reese's life that day but died herself seven days later in the hospital from the virus. Before she died, she managed to infect her entire family and the office where she works. Within a week, half of them were dead. It's a miracle that Reese is alive today."

"Wow," I said.

All these people had rushed to save my sister, but most of them had ended up getting the virus from her, and a lot had died. I looked at Reese and saw the shame on her face. This was a lot to bear for anyone, let alone someone as fragile as my sister.

"But what's really interesting," Al said as she let her fingers dance across the keyboard, "Look at this guy here, wearing a cap pushed down into his face. He entered the supermarket right after Reese did, and he walked right behind her, staying at a distance, but like he was following her, look. He's here, and here, and there. But more than that. I found some other footage from the days before this happened, here, where you see Reese walking downtown. Look who is a few feet behind her as she talks to someone here. Or when she buys a sandwich from this vendor here —look who is standing across the street, looking at her if we use a different camera with another angle; here, look. And the day before, when Reese went to her job at CVS, he came in around noon, then walked up and talked to her, look."

Al zoomed closer in on the guy, but we couldn't really see his face. It wasn't very good quality, and it became blurry pretty fast.

"Looks to me like he was following you, am I right?" Al said and looked at Reese. "And it also kind of looks like you two know each other."

I stared at the picture of him and Reese chatting, then at my sister. "What do you remember about this guy?"

Reese stared at the screen, her eyes blank. She shook her head. "He seems familiar, but I can't really…"

"Can you zoom any closer?" I asked.

"I think I have a better picture of him from the street corner," Al said and tapped again, then found another picture that she zoomed in. Once again, it got pixelated and hard to see. But it was still enough for me to realize that not only did Reese know this guy…I did too.

Chapter 25

REESE STARED at the guy on the screen. She felt so confused, yet there was definitely something about his face that rang a bell. There was something about him that was very familiar—almost eerily so.

"Try to remember, Reese," Harry said, sounding like he was losing his patience with her. "Please, try to remember where you met him?"

She looked up at her brother and tried. She really did her best. Yet, she couldn't.

"Was he a client of yours? Was he a regular customer at the pharmacy?" Al asked. "Was that how you met him?"

"I think so," she said.

"But why would he be following you?" Harry asked, sounding agitated now. "Why would Bobby Kay, the famous environmentalist and artist, be following you, Reese Hunter?"

She shook her head. She didn't know. She wished she knew; she wished she had something to tell him and thought like crazy about it, trying so hard to remember. Even his name rang a bell, and there was more to this, she was certain of it, a lot more; she just couldn't really get her thoughts clear enough to create a picture. She couldn't tell her brother what he needed to hear, and it tormented her.

"I don't know."

Harry tapped on his phone and found a picture, then showed it to her. "This is him, right? This is the guy that you talked to and who was following you, right?"

She nodded. It looked a lot like him. Then something hit her. A memory burst into her mind.

"I think that's the guy from the store, yes. I think I remember him now. He came in a couple of times and talked to me. But there's more. I think I know him from somewhere else too. I think I've been to his office. I remember being there with other people too. I remember he was angry and talking about what he called the inequality of our society. How we should blame the one percent, the rich, and how the system kept the masses poor to control them better. But one day, it would change, he said. One day, the masses would rise from the dust, and it would all change. He also said something about how he wanted to be that change, and we should join him."

Reese smiled when realizing she had finally remembered something seemingly important.

"Sounds like the Bobby Kay we know," Al said, "from all his YouTube videos and demonstrations he has arranged over the years."

"Wait," Harry said and looked at Reese intensely. "Was he also the guy that attacked you last night? You said you saw his eyes but wasn't sure where you had seen them before? Is this him, Reese?"

Reese stared at the picture again, trying to remember his eyes. She couldn't see them in the picture. Were they the same eyes that she had seen the night before, staring down at her while holding a knife to her throat? Were they the same eyes she had seen in her hallucinations?

"I...it might be," she said.

"But you're not sure?" Harry asked with a deep frown.

She looked into his eyes. She didn't like disappointing him. He had been so nice to her through all this. He had believed her and taken her in, then made sure she got her medicine, even though she had been away for so long, completely ignoring him and dodging his calls. Even though she had a baby without telling him, still, he hadn't been angry with her. Shocked, yes, but he never yelled like most men she met. Heck, he'd always been so good to her. He had been taking good care of her all through her life, and she was sick of feeling ashamed of herself because she couldn't remember things when he asked. She really wanted to be able to help him, and even though she had her doubts, she was fairly sure.

"No, I think it's him," she said. "I'm pretty sure it is him."

Harry's frown turned into a smile. Reese enjoyed seeing that. It made her feel calm and like she was useful— that she was finally contributing something. She loved her younger brother dearly. They had always been close, and she had realized just how badly she had missed having him in her life. When Harry was around, everything was good or would be soon enough. He had that ability to always float on top, no matter how badly life wanted to push him down and drown him.

He got up and looked at her.

"Thank you, Reese. You have no idea how big of a help you've just been."

Harry looked at his phone and went to the kitchen for a few minutes, reading something on it, then looked at her, his eyes lighting up. Harry then said he needed to step out for a little while and rushed to the door. Reese glared after him, wanting desperately to ask him… What about Abby? What about the baby? But it was too late.

He had left.

She slumped her shoulders and closed her eyes briefly, listening to her baby's cries, wondering if they only existed in her mind or if she was lying somewhere desperately crying for her mother.

Chapter 26

I KNOCKED ON THE DOOR, then waited. The shops in the strip mall were all closed up with shutters and plywood, reminding me of the few times I had experienced Miami being evacuated when expecting a hurricane. It was odd how you changed your perspective on things when something bad happened. Suddenly, a hurricane seemed like a walk in the park compared to what we were going through. At least we'd know it would have an end at some point. Once the hurricane had passed, we'd do everything to return to normal, and it would happen pretty fast. It lasted a week—maybe two—before things were back to normal, and we'd go about our lives again, soon forgetting it was even here. This virus seemed to go on forever, and there was no end in sight. No one could promise us that we'd be back to our everyday lives within even a month or maybe five. Who knew how long we'd have to stay isolated and scared inside our houses?

It took a while before anything happened on the other side of the door, and I was trying to peek in through a crack in the shutters when the door was opened. A young woman wearing a mask peeked out. Her green eyes lingered on me. She had a very light Eastern European accent when she spoke.

"Yes?"

"Is this OUTRAGED's headquarters?"

The girl nodded cautiously, looking at me suspiciously. I showed her my badge. "I'm Detective Harry Hunter, Miami PD. I'm here to see Bobby Kay. He wrote to me and told me to meet him at this address."

"Can I ask what it's about?" she asked. "Bobby is keeping himself isolated and prefers not to see anyone due to the virus."

"It's about his sister," I said. "Candice Smith."

She didn't budge and kept staring at me like I was the virus itself and had come knocking to kill them all.

A voice yelled behind her, "Let him in, Petra."

Petra stepped aside, and I walked in, careful to remain at least six feet from her at all times. Inside, I was met by two other sets of eyes staring suspiciously back at me. I smiled behind the mask, then nodded in greeting. The walls were decorated with graffiti and posters for their demonstrations. On the back wall, someone had made a huge painting of a homeless man begging in the street, holding up a sign saying *I don't want coins. I want change.*

On another wall, they had created a mural of children's crying faces under a sign saying NO FUTURE.

"I'd shake your hand or fist bump you, but well… these days," a guy said, coming closer but staying six feet from me, "you can't even do that."

"Bobby Kay?" I asked, recognizing him from the articles I had read about him online. Whether this was the same guy on the surveillance videos, the one following Reese, I was less certain. There were similarities, but the guy had worn a cap pulled down on his face, covering his eyes and the top part of his face. I also couldn't tell if it was him I had fought the night before at my house.

"Guilty as charged," he said.

I could tell he was smiling behind his mask due to the small lines shaping around his eyes. He was in his mid-twenties, about ten years younger than me. "What can I do for you? As you can tell, we're closed for the time being. We're not breaking any rules since we're only four people in here, me, Petra, Jacob, and Jim." The other three nodded at me, even though their eyes seemed suspicious of me being there. They seemed like the type who were always suspicious of the police and authority in general. "We're never more than just us these days," Bobby Kay continued. "We have canceled all meetings and demonstrations for now."

"So, what are you doing here?" I asked. "Why aren't you at home?"

"We're planning for the future. As soon as this blows over, they're going to need us more than ever. With all the people who are being laid off, inequality is going to be more visible than ever in society. People will be ready to rise up against their oppressors. We believe revolution is on the way, and we'll help them rise. It's time for the people to do the talking."

I looked at the guy in front of me with an exhale. I couldn't help but think about Al and the weapons on her dining room table.

"So, what can I help you with, Detective?" Bobby Kay said. "You wrote that it had to do with my sister?"

I nodded toward a chair. "Can I sit?"

"Be our guest," Bobby Kay said.

We both sat.

"So, what about my sister?" he asked. He sounded concerned.

"She's missing," I said. "I've been trying to get ahold of you to tell you about her."

"I'm not that easy to find," he said. "Lots of people would love to see me dead. I get threats every day, so I keep to myself and only come out when my presence is needed. So, what happened to my sister?"

"We don't know yet. Apparently, there was a guy in the apartment across the street who saw her being attacked in her condo. He called us, and we went to talk to her, but she wasn't there. There was no sign of forced entry, though, and we didn't find any evidence that he was telling the truth. So, if you can shed any light on where she might be, if she could have left town or if you know where she is, then we'd be most grateful."

"Well, I hardly think she could have left town since we're all on lockdown, and it's not easy to get in and out," Bobby Kay said. "But I'm afraid that's all I can help you with. My sister and I aren't very close. We never talk. To be honest, we barely know one another anymore."

"So, you wouldn't know what happened to her?" I asked.

"I'm afraid not, Detective. But I have to say I am quite worried about her now. I hope she's all right."

I bit my lip, wondering about the surveillance footage of him tailing my sister. I decided I had to ask.

"There was one more thing."

I found my sister's picture on my phone, then turned it to show him.

"Do you know this woman?"

He stared at it, scrutinizing it. "I think I do. I've seen her face on TV. Isn't she the one they said was the first one to get the virus, patient zero?"

I nodded. It was true. All the news stations had run the story of my sister, using an old photo of her. It made me so angry because now she'd be that person for the rest of her life—the face of the Florida Flu.

"Yes, that's her," I said. "Have you ever met her?"

He nodded. "As a matter of fact, I have. She works at the CVS where I get my medications. I have asthma, and that's why I am terrified of getting this virus since it attacks the respiratory system. But, yes, she works there and, in the beginning, when I first saw her photo on TV, I was so scared that she had infected me. I had regular panic attacks at home and felt like I couldn't breathe. But luckily, I didn't get it from her. A lot of others did, though."

"Can you tell me anything about her?" I asked, leaving the part about her being my sister out of the conversation.

"Why? Has she gotten herself in trouble since she got out of the hospital?"

I looked at him, then realized he had no way of knowing she had been discharged. It hadn't been reported in any media outlets. Everything about this guy rubbed me the wrong way for some reason.

"No, no, not at all," I said. "We're just still contract tracing, and, in case you knew her, we'd have to isolate you."

He gave me a look. "A tad too late, don't you think? I mean, if she had infected me, then I'd be sick by now, don't you think?"

"Just trying to be safe," I said and got up. "Anyway, thank you for your time. I'll show myself out."

Chapter 27

CANDICE FELT the drops of sweat as they sprang to her forehead. It was hot in the room where she was being kept. It seemed hotter than usual. She wondered for a second if her captor had left and turned off the AC to let her die in the heat. Candice knew that she was somewhere remote because she never heard sounds coming from outside the room. Not even the engine of a car or the rumbling of a train. There were no voices outside the door or footsteps to indicate there was human life around her. It was all so quiet.

Too quiet.

And time seemed to pass so slowly. She was tired of thinking, of wondering what her captor wanted with her. It couldn't be rape because he'd have done it by now, and he had barely touched her all this time. But she couldn't for the life of her figure out why else he'd kidnap her and keep her like this. Why not just kill her right away if that was the plan? And why had he attached the bomb to the door? Was it her guard? To make sure she didn't try and get out? She came to the conclusion that was probably it. He feared she might get loose somehow, and then run away. But wouldn't he have warned her, then? Told her *don't try to escape or you'll be blown to smithereens?*

She kept thinking about his voice. It was familiar somehow, but she hadn't come up with where she had heard it. She had been on so many blind dates. It could be any of them, she thought. But he had said something about her thinking about what she had done, and that stuck with her.

What had she done to deserve this treatment?

Candice felt thirst nagging at the back of her throat and wondered when he would be back…if he ever would. That was when she heard the first sound in days…a rattling behind the door and she held her breath.

Was it him? Was it someone else?

If so, then they wouldn't know about the bomb and how to disable it. If they came in here, then they'd both be gone.

Oh, dear God, please, let it be him.

There were more jangling noises behind the door, and she heard it open slowly. She held her breath again, wondering if this was the moment it would all end for her, waiting for the massive blast.

But nothing came.

Everything was silent until she heard footsteps approaching, and someone knelt next to her. She could hear his breathing close to her face and started to breathe raggedly herself. Fingers moved behind her neck as the gag was removed. Then she felt the familiar feeling of a plastic bottle being pressed against her lips and water hitting her tongue. Then she drank. Greedily, she gulped down the water.

As the plastic bottle was removed, a piece of bread came against her lips, and she bit into it, taking huge bites that she could barely chew.

"Why are you keeping me here?" she asked between bites. She sounded like a broken record since she had asked him this repeatedly. Her blindfold was still lifted slightly at the bottom, and she could see his red sneakers.

"Please. Just let me go. Please," she added. "What did I ever do to you? I never hurt you or anyone else."

She felt him close to her face again. She could feel a beard or at least stubble as it scratched against her skin. Then he whispered:

"You thought you could play God, didn't you? You created this virus, Candice. You're to blame for all this."

Chapter 28

"I THINK he was lying through his teeth."

I looked down at Al. She was sitting in her chair at her computer. Reese was on the couch, taking a nap while I told Al everything about Candice and her disappearance. She was still exhausted from being hospitalized for a long time and needed rest. Her lungs had been damaged by this vicious virus, and the doctors hadn't been able to tell her if it would ever get better—if she'd ever fully recuperate. It was tough when you knew so little about a virus and its effects.

Al nodded pensively. She clicked the mouse a few times, then showed me something. "I think you're right. Look what I found. It took me literally one second."

I stared at the pictures. They showed Candice standing with Bobby Kay on a boat. He was holding a huge fish he had just caught, and, in the caption, it said they were in Key West.

"I just found these on her Instagram account," Al said. "They're from last year about this same time."

"Barely know each other, huh?" I asked as Al scrolled

through other pictures and showed me all of them, arm in arm or heads close together, faces smiling, captions reading stuff like *Having a brother is like having your very own superhero*, or *Like sugar and spice, a brother makes everything nice.*

I shook my head in disbelief. "I knew he was lying to me when he said that. I could see it in his eyes. But why? Why would he try to hide his relationship with his sister?"

"Because he knows something he's not telling you?" Al said.

I nodded. "Exactly."

I exhaled and went for some iced tea in the fridge. Today, it was extremely hot outside and humid, too— typical Florida Spring.

Al was staring at her screen, her fingers tapping the keyboard while I enjoyed my cold drink. I looked at my sleeping sister, wondering whether she truly was healed from this awful virus or not. Then I thought with deep sadness about our dad, and how he was holding up at the house. What was I going to do if he got so bad that he couldn't breathe? I had read about people who suffered so terribly they couldn't even walk from the bed to the bathroom. There was nowhere I could take him if that happened. What if he needed to go to the hospital? Would I take him there and pray they'd take him? I had seen a news report about the thousands who were turned away just this past week because there was no room for them. They had put up huge tents in the parks closest to the hospitals, but that had just become another place for people to come and die. They had no ventilators for them. They were all being used for kids. There was a devastating interview with the daughter of an eighty-year-old woman, who cried and said she didn't even get to say goodbye to her own mother. She died in that tent, all alone, surrounded only by others who were sick. I never wanted that to happen to my dad. I'd much rather have him die at home in my house.

Even though it was a risk for both Josie and me, I couldn't just send him off to one of those places to die from this awful virus, all alone.

"You're not going to believe it," Al said and leaned back in her chair. She glared at me and took off her glasses for the first time since we got there. "I think we're onto something here, Hunter. Something big."

Chapter 29

I PULLED up a chair and sat next to Al, yet maintaining distance, while she showed me what she had found.

"I did a little research on Candice Smith," she said. "And this is what I found."

She scrolled down and stopped, so I could see her picture properly, then pointed at the text below. "She is a molecular biologist and director of the lab of antiviral mechanisms at the US Army Research, USAMRIID, Institute on Infectious Diseases. USAMRIID has served as the Department of Defense's lead laboratory for medical biological defense research since the sixties. Among other things, they investigate disease outbreaks and threats to public health. Candice Smith has been involved in the development of vaccines to protect against biological threats like Anthrax and Ebola. She is pretty famous within those circles and rather criticized for a lot of her work. According to what I've read here, she unearthed the passageways for viruses to enter the human body. She successfully isolated three viruses from snakes that she experimented on in a lab, supposedly so we'd know more about a virus like it should we ever have a pandemic. All was done in the attempt to be able to create a vaccine quickly. But she didn't stop there. Recently, she published a paper discussing the creation of a synthetic virus. Used on mice, it showed lung damage, and then when she moved on to subjecting it to primates, monkeys, it killed all the children within days and severely damaged the lungs of the adults, some of them who died later. This was when the world of virologists began to express deep concern. Other scientists wrote about her in scientific magazines, discussing her work in a heated debate. A French scientist wrote that if this new virus escaped, no one could project the damage it might do or what tragedies might follow. That was three years ago."

Al turned to look at me, leaning back in her chair.

"It doesn't take a genius detective to realize something fishy is going on here," she added.

I stared at her, a million thoughts rushing through my mind, then looked at the screen. I knew that Candice was a biologist, but this was beyond anything I had been able to imagine.

"So, you think she created the virus?" I asked, rubbing my hair.

"Sure sounds like it," Al said.

"And that's why she's missing?"

Al shrugged. "Your guess is as good as mine. She might have made herself disappear because it was her fault that it escaped the lab. She might have gone into hiding."

"Except her boyfriend saw her being attacked in her apartment," I said pensively. "And carried to a car, unconscious from what he could see."

"Okay, so let's assume she was kidnapped."

"But why? Because of the virus she created?" I asked.

"Maybe the government realized they're to blame for

this, if it was created in an army research lab, and are trying to cover it up," Al said. "Maybe they have removed her to make sure she doesn't tell the truth. Think of the repercussions that would follow if the world found out the US Army was behind this misery. Millions of people are out of work, people are going hungry, and the economy has completely crashed due to this worldwide lockdown. Not to mention all the people that have died, most of them children. It could get really ugly."

I leaned back in the chair, feeling stirred up inside. So much about this felt so wrong. If Al was right, there probably wasn't much I could do to find Candice. But what about my sister? What about Reese? Why was Candice's brother trying to silence her? How did he know she was out of the hospital? And what was even more confusing was the question of her baby. Did she play a role in this mystery? And where the heck was she?

Chapter 30

WHEN I WAS AT HOME LATER that night, cooking dinner, my partner Propper called.

"Just checking in to see how you're holding up," he said. "I'm getting kind of bored around the house, going stir crazy, you know?"

I exhaled, holding the phone between my shoulder and ear while shaping the meatballs. I wanted to tell him that I wished that was my biggest problem right now, and not the fear for my dad's and daughter's lives, or my sister for that matter. If all I had to worry about was going stir crazy, that would be awesome. I had heard people complaining about this lockdown for so long, especially on social media, where they shared recipes and showed themselves drinking wine at ten in the morning. It rubbed me the wrong way when thinking about Jean, who was at the hospital for hours on end, fighting for the lives affected by this. Jean, who fought for others, risking her own life, barely having time even to eat. I exhaled deeply and looked toward her house next to mine. It was screamingly empty. Gosh, I missed her. I missed holding her in my arms so terribly and wondered if I would ever get to again.

"It's getting to us all, I guess," I said, keeping my opinions to myself. "And I'm sorry for being the reason you can't go to work. But you're well?"

"Yes, I'm fine. How's your dad doing?"

I paused as my dad had another coughing attack. I could hear him wheezing in his room, fighting even to breathe. It wasn't getting any better, and my stomach churned with worry.

"Not that good, I'm afraid."

"I'm sorry to hear that, my friend. I truly am."

I sniffled and stared at my hands, smeared with meat. "Thanks, man. I appreciate it."

"But the reason I called is also that I have received news in the Candice Smith case."

My eyes grew wide, and I grabbed the phone in my hand.

"You did what?"

"Yes. Major Walker called. He said that her brother called earlier today and told them she was with him. It was all just a misunderstanding. She was sick, and that was why he came to get her at her apartment and carried her out to the car. He had her at his house, where she was hopefully recovering. So, Walker has dismissed the case."

I bit my cheek, wondering about this new information. It made no sense except if Bobby Kay wanted the police off his back. But why? If he had nothing to hide?

"Thanks for the information," I said.

"I thought it might bring some relief in this difficult time to know that she's fine. I know how much into the case you were."

"Yes, yes," I said absentmindedly. "I was. Thanks."

"No problem. Take care."

"You too."

I pressed my screen to hang up, then stood for a few minutes, wondering about this. I finished making the spaghetti and meatballs, then rushed upstairs to Josie's room and placed the tray outside her room and knocked.

There was no answer.

Concerned at this, I knocked again.

Still, no answer.

"Josie?" I called and knocked harder, almost hammering desperately on the door. "Josie?"

Finally, the door opened. A sleepy Josie peeked out, and I stepped back to remain at a distance.

"What? Why are you pounding on my door? It's annoying, Dad."

I breathed with relief. "I was just…I'm sorry. I wanted to let you know that dinner is ready, and you weren't answering."

Her tired eyes stared at me. "I fell asleep. How long have I slept? What time is it? Is it dinnertime already?"

I tilted my head and looked at her, my pulse quickening. I didn't like the sound of this. It scared me senseless. Had she turned her days and nights upside down, or was there more to it than that?

"Are you okay, Josie?"

"Yeah…well, now that you mention it, I do feel kind of achy. My body is hurting. My muscles are really sore."

I was barely breathing at this point. Her eyes were moist, her cheeks blushing, and she was breathing heavily.

"Josie, do you have a fever? Do you think you might have a fever? Please, Josie, talk to me."

"I'm not sure," she said, closing her eyes briefly. "I feel really tired, Dad. Can't I just go back to sleep?"

I shook my head. "No. Not now. I'll get you a thermometer, and then I want you to take your temperature, you hear me?"

I rushed into the bathroom and searched through my stuff, then found a thermometer, the one I usually used for Josie. We each have one, so we don't have to share. I hurried back and handed it to her. She stuck it under her tongue, and then we waited, her leaning on the door.

It beeped, and my heart was racing as she pulled it out of her mouth.

"What does it say?"

She wrinkled her forehead. She looked at the display again, then blinked her eyes. "This can't be right."

"What do you mean?" I asked petrified. "What does it say, Josie? Josie? What does it say on the display?"

She looked up and into my eyes. I could barely breathe; that's how scared I felt at this moment.

"A hundred and two?" she said. "That's bad, isn't it, Dad?"

I swallowed hard.

"Yes, sweetie. That's bad. That's really bad."

Chapter 31

I RODE with Josie in the ambulance. It was Doctor Bird who told me we had to take her in straight away due to her heart condition. Josie had a heart transplant only a few months earlier and running a high fever with the risk of it being the virus, she needed the best care she could get. She was a high-risk patient.

The road to the hospital was completely empty, so it wasn't a long drive. The paramedics ran to the back and opened the doors, then rolled Josie out of the ambulance. I barely made it out of the back before I saw her being taken inside. A nurse stopped me right in front of the door when I tried to follow. She was wearing a full body suit, gloves, and a clear plastic shield covered her face.

"I'm sorry, sir. No visitors allowed at the hospital," she said, barely looking at me.

"But...but my daughter was just rolled in and...? Surely, she can't be in there all by herself?"

"I'm sorry, sir. There's nothing I can do."

I stood there as the doors slid shut, and the nurse in the blue suit disappeared. Suddenly, everything went completely quiet around me, and I realized how empty the streets and the parking lot in front of the hospital were.

Was this it?

What if she dies in there all by herself? What if I don't even get to say goodbye? She must be terrified.

I know I was. I hadn't been this scared since she fainted in our backyard and had to have the heart transplant. I grabbed my phone and called Jean.

"Hello there, handsome," she said. I was lucky that she picked up. Over the past few weeks, I hadn't been able to reach her when I tried.

"Jean. Josie was just taken to the ICU. She has a fever, a high one. I'm scared."

Jean went quiet on the other end. When she finally spoke, it was barely a whisper.

"Oh, dear God, no."

"I don't know what to do. They won't let me go in with her. Can't you help me?"

"I'm sorry, Harry. They're not letting any parents in. We have all these poor kids fighting for their lives, and their parents can't be with them. A lot of them don't even get to say goodbye. Earlier today, I Facetimed a mother so she could say goodbye to her twelve-year-old son. It was heart-breaking; you have no idea."

That wasn't exactly what I wanted to hear at this point, and my heart sank. I felt like screaming.

"I'm sorry," Jean said. "That was inconsiderate of me. I'm sure Josie will be all right. Some patients are getting better now. We will see lots of recovering patients soon; I'm certain of it. Your sister recovered, remember?"

"But so far, she's the only one," I said. "And Josie has a weak heart."

"But many are getting better," Jean said again to make sure I heard it. "At least, we hope they are. I have two patients this morning whose oxygen numbers improved from yesterday. I feel confident—and so does the doctor, by the way—that those two will make it. You mustn't lose hope, Harry. The doctors here are getting good at taking care of the patients. We're learning new things about the virus every day. You must keep your faith, Harry. You must trust that God will come through for you and Josie. He's done it before, remember?"

I exhaled, reminding myself of how Josie had fought for her life when she suffered heart failure and how there had been no new heart for her, but still, we found one, and she was saved at the last minute. I knew God had taken care of her back then, and, of course, He'd do it again.

"You're right," I said. "Thanks. I needed that."

I hung up, feeling slightly better, but still scared like crazy. I felt such deep anger toward this virus and how it had destroyed my life. That was when I decided to turn my anger toward those responsible.

Chapter 32

MUCH TO MY SURPRISE, Bobby Kay lived in one of the most affluent neighborhoods in Miami, with views over Biscayne Bay. Al helped me find his address through the DMV database, and she texted it to me. Furious, I drove there, then as I found the right house, my jaw just about dropped. The house was a brand-new three-story white luxury mansion with a flat roof and floor-to-ceiling panoramic windows. It made no sense to me. How did a guy who fought for more equality in society…how did he live like this? Was Bobby Kay one of the one percent?

I drove up the driveway and got out, completely overwhelmed by this. It only confirmed my suspicion that something was very fishy about this organization, and especially about Bobby Kay.

I rang the doorbell, then knocked on the wooden door, hard.

Jacob, one of the guys who had been in the back at the headquarters, opened the door.

"Detective Hunter," he said. "What on earth are you doing here?"

"I need to see Bobby Kay," I said. "I have something I need to talk to him about."

He scoffed. "Well, you can't."

"Why not?"

Jacob smirked. "He doesn't want to see you."

I lifted my badge and held it up. "Will he see me now?"

That made Jacob laugh. "No, he won't. He's sick, and so is his sister. We believe they have caught the virus and need to keep them away from people. They've been quarantined."

I wrinkled my forehead. This was very sudden.

"Bobby Kay is sick?"

"Yes, that's what I just told you. That's why you can't see him. We can't risk infecting anyone. You, of all people, should know the rules, Detective. Besides, aren't you supposed to be in quarantine as well? That's what I heard. To be honest, this doesn't look good. You shouldn't be running around out here infecting people when you have a sick family member at home. You shouldn't be breaking your quarantine."

I narrowed my eyes.

"How do you know about that?"

"Bobby Kay called your station and talked to Major Walker. He told us something very interesting. He said you weren't on duty, that you were staying home because you had a father who had come down with the virus and that you were also quarantined. As far as I can see, this is the second time you're breaking that quarantine, Detective. You want me to call the major and let him know you've been out infecting people, abusing your power?"

I stared at the guy in front of me, not knowing what to say. He was right. I had broken all the rules by taking Reese to Al's place and by going to their headquarters. There was nothing I could say to justify it.

"I didn't think so," he said. "Let's just say you're going to leave, and then we won't talk anymore about this."

He smiled an unfriendly smile, and as he was about to close the door, I heard a baby cry in the background. The sound came from inside the house. My heart skipped a beat, and I was about to ask about it.

"What is…"

But Jacob didn't wait for me to finish the sentence before he shut the door in my face. I stood by the closed door, my hands shaking violently in anger. Was that Abby I had heard?

Had these people taken Reese's baby?

Chapter 33

REESE WAS awake when I got back to Al's place. I kept my phone close in case they called from the hospital. Jean had promised to keep an eye on Josie and make sure she got the treatment she needed. I was too terrified even to think about my daughter and how she was doing. Driven by anger toward those responsible, I rushed up to Al.

"I want to know everything about this group, about OUTRAGED, about Bobby Kay and those that work for him," I said. "Who are they? Where do they come from? How do they know one another, where do they get their money? Everything there is to know about them."

"I'm on it," Al said and threw herself at the keyboard. I turned to face Reese, then sat down on the couch with her.

"How are you feeling?" I asked.

"I'm doing pretty okay," she said, looking confused. "I would kill for a cup of coffee, though."

"I can fix that," I said as I got up and walked into Al's small kitchen.

Al had already made a pot, and I poured us each a

cup. I tasted it quickly to make sure it was drinkable. Al tended to buy these strange types of coffee that, for the most part, tasted awful, but this one seemed pretty normal. The aftertaste was nutty, but I could live with that.

I handed Reese the cup, and she took it, sending me a look of gratitude. She held the cup between both her hands while sipping it. She closed her eyes briefly, then looked up at me.

"Just what I needed."

I drank too. I had added a lot of sugar to make sure it tasted the way I liked it. I preferred my coffee sweet.

"I went to see Bobby Kay," I said after a few seconds of silence. I was pondering how much to tell her. I didn't want to get her hopes up too high. I had heard a baby cry, yes, but that could be any baby. It could be Bobby Kay's or one of his co-worker's. It could be visiting.

But it could also be Abby.

"Oh?" she said and looked up at me. "Why?"

"He claims his sister is at his house, and I wanted to see her, to make sure she was all right. But they're both sick, according to the guy who opened the door, and they wouldn't let me come in."

Reese looked down at her feet, then shook her head. "I think I remember something more. I think I remember the day she was taken from me."

I put down my cup.

"Really?"

She nodded, stifling her tears. "I'm not sure, but I keep seeing this woman coming in through my door, but she isn't alone. There are two men with her, and they take Abby. They knock on my door, and I go to open it, then they go directly for the baby, who is lying in her carrier. I scream and cry for them not to, but they lift her up and simply leave with her. I plead and cry, but they do it anyway."

Reese's eyes met mine. Hers were filling. "Why would anyone take my baby, Harry? Why?"

I placed my hand on her arm and looked straight into her eyes. "Was it Bobby Kay who took her? Try to think, Reese. Was he there on the day they took her?"

She shook her head, the tears spilling onto her cheeks. "I don't know. I can't remember their faces."

"Okay," I said, mustering all the patience I could. "Let's try something else. Did you call the police when they took Abby?"

Reese thought for a second, then shook her head. "I don't believe so."

"Why didn't you call the police if someone took your child, Reese?" I asked, worried deeply. Something was so wrong about this. I knew that when Reese was off her meds, life was a little like a dream to her, and she couldn't keep her thoughts from one another; everything sort of melted together in her mind. That was how our old doctor used to explain it to our parents, and it was the best way for me to understand what it was like for her. It was just so frustrating that she didn't remember more. It was in there somewhere. We both knew it was. It was just a question of accessing it. I knew that pressuring her didn't work. It took time, a lot of time. I wasn't sure I had that kind of patience.

She swallowed. Her eyes flickered back and forth in confusion.

"I...I don't know."

"Did they blackmail you, Reese? Did they ask you to do something to get the baby back?"

"I...I...don't..."

"Think, Reese. Was there something they told you to do? Something you didn't want to, but you had to?"

"Like what? What are you talking about, Harry?"

"Did they ask you to steal something, maybe from a lab? And then promised you'd get Abby back if you did it?"

"Steal something? Like what?"

I shrugged. "I don't know. Maybe a sample of a virus?"

"I...I..."

"Think, Reese. Please try and remember what Bobby Kay talked to you about. Just something he might have told you? Anything? Did you go to his house? Did he come to you? How often did you two talk?"

Her eyes were blank, and I knew the answer before it left her lips.

"I don't know! I don't know, Harry. I don't remember. I'm not lying to you. I can't recall it, no matter how hard I try. Please, stop asking, Harry; it hurts my head!"

"Okay, okay," I said, trying to calm her. "Maybe you'll remember a little later. But please, try all you can. I have a feeling that the solution to all this mess lies with Abby and what happened to her."

Reese nodded. "I'm trying, Harry. It's all I do."

I smiled gently. I didn't want her to feel worse than she already did. I squeezed her arm.

"That's good, Reese. That's really good."

"Oh, dear God," Al suddenly exclaimed from her seat. She took off her headset and turned to look at me. "I think I found something."

Chapter 34

AL PRINTED out some pictures and placed them on the desk in front of me, creating what looked like an organizational structure for OUTRAGED. She put Bobby Kay at the top, then pointed at his picture.

"Robert Kay Smith, brother to Candice Smith. Bobby is an artist and a poet and the guy in charge of this organization. He started the protest group in two thousand and fourteen, as a running club. People ran to collect money for charity, or in protest of the oppression of the poorest in society, the single mother who works three jobs, the homeless, the children in foster care, and so on. All in all, a very noble cause. He's known in the media for saying things as they are, and he's known as what they call a creative influencer. He reaches millions of people through his YouTube Videos, and when he did a night run in protest against the death penalty, more than ten thousand people showed up. They call him the marathon man or the running man, and he has been named by *People Magazine* as one of the *New century role models for men*."

"Okay," I said. "What about on the personal level. Is he married? Does he have children?"

"No. He's a very sought-after bachelor. Especially the affluent Miami girls who want to outrage their daddies like to date him and show him off in the papers or magazines. But their relationships don't seem to last long—probably because he doesn't approve of their lifestyles. One girl was quoted saying that Bobby Kay wanted her to donate half of all her money to charity if they were to stay together. She called it blackmail and left."

I looked at Reese, thinking about this. What exactly was her connection to them? I was annoyed that I didn't get to talk to Bobby Kay earlier in the day since I desperately wanted to ask him about her again.

"What else? Where did he come from? How did he get this social indignation and outrage? Why is he fighting for these causes?"

"That's what I find slightly odd," Al said. "He's an ordinary kid from a middle-class home outside Milwaukee, Wisconsin. Parents aren't even divorced. Went to public school but a good one in a decent middle-class neighborhood. I don't find anything here to tell me why he would fight for equality with such passion."

"It could have happened later in life," I said. "People he met when coming to Miami, maybe from living as a starving artist."

"But I get the feeling he never really did fit into that picture of being a starving artist," Al said.

"I saw his house," I said. "Where does he get the money?"

"The money belongs to Jacob and Petra Lebedev," Al said and pointed at their pictures.

"They're married?"

Al shook her head. "Siblings, actually they're twins.

Parents were Russian and moved here when the twins were just one year old, and they all became citizens."

"And where did they get the money?" I asked. "They can't be more than twenty-five years old?"

"Twenty-four, actually. They got the money when they turned eighteen. On their eighteenth birthdays, they each received almost a hundred million dollars from their parents' foundation. Their names are on the lease for the headquarters downtown. Last year, they bought the house where they all live now. They met Bobby Kay at an artist event in two thousand and fourteen and have supported his happenings ever since. A few months later, he created OUTRAGED."

"What happened to the twins' parents?" I asked.

"Their parents died when the twins were just five years old. Got shot in their own home here in Miami. Drug-related, the police concluded, but the shooter was never found, and it was never proven that their parents were part of the Russian drug cartel. The money waited for the children to be released once they were old enough. Here. You can read more about them in these articles. I also found their files in the DCF database. Here."

I lifted my gaze to her.

"DCF?"

"Yes," Al said, nodding. "They were both placed in foster care after their parents died. Since the money wasn't accessible till they were eighteen, and since there were no relatives to be found anywhere, they went through a lot of families and didn't seem to fit anywhere. They were also separated for many years."

I grabbed the papers she had printed and skimmed through them, thinking I'd take a closer look later, maybe once I got home. I needed something to keep my mind off the fact that my daughter was in the hospital and that I couldn't see her and the fact that my dad was fighting for his life in the back room and I couldn't do anything about it. I knew I wasn't going to get any sleep tonight, and these files could keep me busy, so I wouldn't overthink. I felt a great urge to punish those responsible for this virus, and my theory was that Bobby Kay and his gang had something to do with it; I just couldn't quite figure out how or what. I had spent a lot of energy thinking about this for most of the day. All day, I had also been wondering about Camille, my ex-wife. She was in the witness protection program and had changed her identity. I had no idea where she was in the world, and naturally, I wondered what would happen if Josie died. How would I let her know? She had to find out somehow, right? Was there someone in the FBI that could get me in touch with her? Was there a way of tracing her? They had to have some paperwork on her, a casefile, or something, right?

I prayed I never needed to find out.

"So now we have an explanation for the twins' indignation toward the system and society in general. Who else is there?"

Al pointed at the last picture. I recognized the guy in it from when I had been at the headquarters, sitting in the back by a laptop computer. His eyes had stared at me, and it felt like there had been so much anger in them; it was uncomfortable. I guessed that, to him, I symbolized everything he was against. Authority. The system. Society. I had seen that look of distrust many times before.

"There's Jim—or James Hudson. He's also one of the core members and on the payroll of the organization. He's also been a member pretty much from the beginning. James grew up in a suburb of New York and lost his mother when he was ten years old. His dad didn't want him, so he was adopted into another family who later left him at the local fire station because they couldn't take care of him. He spent his teenage years at a home for troubled children. Later, he started writing for these underground magazines before the organization hired him as their press secretary. He writes their press releases and takes care of their social media accounts and so on. He might have written this on behalf of Bobby."

Al placed a printout in front of me. She pushed it across the table, so she wouldn't have to get too close to me.

"What's this?" I asked. I looked down at it, then back up at her.

"A manifesto that I found in an online forum. It was written by Bobby Kay about two years ago but has suddenly become very current. I'll let you read it, and then you can tell me what you think."

Chapter 35

CANDICE WAS CRYING behind the blindfold. Not so much because of the situation, she was crying over that too, but it was also something else. What had gotten to her was what the captor had said the last time he was with her, when he was feeding her. He had whispered in her ear that she was to blame for all the mess the world had ended in.

That it was her virus.

Hearing him say it the way he did had thrown her into a deep sadness that she couldn't shake. She kept crying, soaking the blindfold because he was right. She cried because it was the truth. She had avoided thinking about it for weeks, while staying in her condo, isolated from the world, only keeping track of what was going on through the news and social media. She had been telling herself it wasn't her fault, that she couldn't have helped it, that all she did was research, which was her job. But as she sat on the mattress on the floor, she finally admitted to herself that it was all her fault, that she was, in fact, to blame. People—kids—were dying because of her—because of what she had done.

She deserved to be treated this way. She deserved to be raped or murdered or both for what she had done.

I'm sorry, God. I'm so, so sorry. Please, forgive me.

She thought she had been onto something big when tampering with the virus. She had been so enthralled by her research that she hadn't even thought about the ethical aspects of creating a virus like this. Well, that wasn't exactly true. Of course, it had lingered in the back of her mind. There had been a voice telling her not to do this. But she had done it anyway. She had discovered the protein this virus was missing, and it had kept her awake at night; that's how excited she had been. Then she had added the S-protein to the virus's DNA and subjected mice to it and later monkeys. It had been thrilling and so breath-taking to be a part of that she hadn't listened when her colleagues had told her it was dangerous. That what she did was unethical. Candice had believed she was on the verge of a great discovery, one that would make her famous, and one that could help save millions of lives. It was the biggest discovery of her career, one that would put her up there with the big names. Of course, she knew it could be used as a weapon if it fell into the wrong hands, but she had never thought it would leave her lab. It wasn't supposed to. She was supposed to write papers on it, study it, and create a vaccine for it, and nothing more. It should have stayed within the lab.

So, what happened?

She still didn't know how it escaped. She just knew that once the first patients were admitted and the talk about a new unknown virus started, she read what the doctors wrote about it in their reports. She still remembered the feeling as her blood froze over when realizing this had to be her virus. She had created this monster, and now it was loose. It was beyond her deepest and darkest nightmares.

She had gone home to her apartment, closed the door, and locked it. She hadn't left the place again, except to buy groceries. With quivering lips, she had watched as it ravaged the city and soon the world, fearing someone might find out it was her doing.

And now they had. This guy, her captor, knew the truth.

It was all over.

Her punishment was coming, and she was ready to take it.

Candice sniffled and exhaled as she ran out of tears. Barely had she stopped crying before there was a sound from behind the door and it was opened. She held her breath for a second, wondering if the bomb would go off, in case it wasn't someone who knew how to disable it. But nothing happened. There were footsteps, and someone sat down on the mattress next to her, his shoulder rubbing up against hers.

Candice growled behind the gag, but it wasn't removed like it usually was when she was allowed to drink and eat. Instead, a voice spoke next to her. The sound of it felt like knives to her skin as a great fear welled up inside of her.

"Candice? It's me."

Chapter 36

WE WERE WAITING FOR AL. Reese and I were sitting in my police cruiser in the alley behind her building, the engine running, while she closed everything. Finally, she came down and walked up to us. She was wearing a complete hazmat suit with gasmask and everything as she got inside and sat down in the back, placing a gun on the seat next to her. I turned and stared at her, then shrugged and took off.

"Can't be too careful," she said.

I didn't say anything. I had enough on my mind the way it was. Al was paranoid in general, yes, but with this virus, I couldn't blame her for taking all precautions. I had seen what this bastard had done to my dad in just a few days; I knew it was no joke. Reese knew this too. She had suffered it in her own body and still had trouble breathing properly, so she didn't say anything either. She stared out the window at Miami rushing by. I could tell she was deeply worried, and I hadn't been sure I wanted to bring her along. But I hoped that once she saw the house, or if we were lucky, maybe saw Bobby Kay, then perhaps it would jump-start her memory.

I drove up in the driveway and parked in front of the massive luxury mansion. I turned to look at Reese as I killed the engine, hoping for a reaction—a smile of recognition, or even a wince, anything.

But there was nothing to be seen on her face. She sat completely still and stared at the house out the window.

"You ready?" I asked.

She wrinkled her forehead like she was confused.

"It's okay, Reese," I said. "I'll do the talking."

"So, what exactly are we doing?" Al asked as we got out of the car and walked up to the front door.

I glared at her, unsure what to say. I hadn't exactly made a plan or anything. I just knew that I needed to talk with them after reading the manifesto. I thought about calling Major Walker and letting him deal with it, but if he got involved, he'd find out that I had been breaking my quarantine. I thought I'd better deal with this myself, at least until I had some solid evidence.

I took my phone out of my pocket and looked at the display, then tapped the screen to make sure it was turned on. I hadn't heard anything from the hospital, and it worried me deeply. Still, I reminded myself that no news was good news, right? Jean would most definitely call me if there were anything important going on, anything serious.

Unless they're fighting for her life, then they won't have time to call you till it's too late.

The thought brought unease to my stomach, and I felt like I had to throw up. I closed my eyes briefly and pinched the bridge of my nose while I shook my head. I couldn't think like this. It was out of my hands, but that didn't mean it was over. I had to keep the faith and believe for the best. And then do what I could to bring those responsible to justice.

I lifted my gaze and looked at the door in front of me. In the pocket of my jacket, I had the warrant I had received in my email less than an hour ago. I had pulled some strings with a judge I had known for years and who owed me a favor. He didn't even know I was supposed to be quarantined and didn't ask, so I didn't have to lie to him, which suited me fine.

I took a deep breath, praying for the best outcome, then lifted my fist and knocked.

"Miami PD! Open up."

Chapter 37

NO ONE CAME to open the door. I kept knocking, but nothing happened. Warrant in hand, I walked to the back and found a sliding door that was left unlocked and opened it. I walked in, Reese and Al following me closely, a hand on my gun in the unbuttoned holster.

"Hello? Miami PD. Please, come out if you can hear my voice. Please, come out with your hands above your head."

Nothing. Not a single movement.

I pulled out my gun and walked from room to room, clearing them before I let Reese and Al follow me inside. I stopped in an office, where I found an open laptop among piles of papers and books. Al rushed in behind me and scanned the papers quickly. She held up a document.

"Look at this," she said. "If this isn't incriminating, then I don't know what is."

I walked up behind her and looked at what she was holding. It was a map of Miami and had marked places all over the city. I showed it to Reese.

"What am I looking at here?" she asked.

"These are all places you went in the days after you were infected with the virus. Look, that's your workplace, the CVS, this is the supermarket where you fainted. Bobby Kay knew you were going to all these places because he had told you to, right? So you could infect as many people as possible before you got really sick yourself."

Reese stared at the map, then nodded her head. "You're right; I did go to all these places."

"And we saw Bobby Kay follow you all over town on the surveillance cameras," Al said. "Why would he do that if not to make sure you did as he had told you?"

"He's even written next to them just how many people got infected in those places; look, there are small numbers next to each location," I said and showed it to her. "Here and here."

Reese wrinkled her nose and looked up at me. "So, you're saying they infected me with the virus somehow and then asked me to go all these places to infect as many people as possible?"

I nodded. "I think they stole it from the lab, or maybe Candice gave it to them because she was working with them because of her brother. Then they kidnapped Abby and told you to get infected and spread the virus for them, so it could never be traced to them. That was the only way you could get Abby back. They probably assumed you'd die from it, so they wouldn't have to deal with you anymore afterward, and when you didn't, they tried to kill you in your apartment and my home."

Reese stared at me. I could see small droplets of sweat springing from her forehead.

"Does any of what I'm saying ring a bell, Reese?" I asked. "Any part of it?"

She swallowed hard, then looked up at me, eyes big and wide. "I...I...guess, maybe. I don't know."

She sat down in a leather chair behind her, holding her head between her hands. She was struggling with getting her mind to work properly, and I felt for her. It had to be awful not to know what you had done or what had happened.

"It's okay, Reese," I said and took her hand in mine. "It'll come. It'll come back to you when you're ready."

"But why?" Reese asked. "Why would they do such an awful thing?"

"To create a new world," I said and squatted in front of her to better look into her eyes as I spoke. "That is their goal. If you read their manifesto from two years ago, Bobby Kay talked about creating a new world order where the oppressed rose to rule in a world where there'd be no more poverty, where the wealth of the world would be distributed more evenly. But, as he said, a drastic event was needed to accomplish this goal. He even said in the manifesto that he believed it could happen in many ways; for instance, a pandemic could drastically change the world as we knew it. He said so himself in the manifesto, Reese. He believed this was the way the world could be changed for the better."

"So, you think they'll start a war? Stage a coup to take over when this ends?" Reese asked.

"They have millions of followers on social media," I said. "What if they asked all of them to rise up? If they were preppers like Al, then they'd have weapons and an army. I'm not saying they'd succeed, but it could turn ugly. It might already be too late to stop them."

"As I told you earlier," Al said pensively. "There has been a lot of chatter online among conspiracy theorists that this virus attack was planned. Many—mostly what you'd normally consider wacko conspiracy theorists—are also saying that it marks the beginning of a new era, a new world order, stuff like that. They call it Gesera Nesera. A sort of global reset of the economy."

"I think I heard about this," I said. "Draining the swamps they say too, right? Root out corruption. But what does it mean?"

Al sighed. "Supposedly, it means an end to the leadership and economic systems as we know them. The end of poverty, end of hunger, end of debt—only global peace and prosperity for all. Nesera stands for National Economic Security and Reformation Act, and Gesera is the same, just Global act instead of National. If you read about it, it goes back to the work of St. Germaine in the fifteenth century. It was designed to provide a new economic system for the world during a time of transition. They dream of doing much like what the Nazis and communists did in Europe after the Great Depression— utilize this vacuum to rise to power. They believe that our leaders have already declared war on our constitution by removing our constitutional rights, like freedom of assembly, freedom to travel, the right to earn a living, the right to freely worship, and so on. They have violated their constitutional oath, and so forfeited their office and authority. These people are not kidding around. They have been waiting for a chance like this for years, and they're ready. I've read talks about storming the state capitol. They're like racehorses in the box, waiting for the start signal. This virus could be the signal they have been waiting for."

"That's insane," I said. "The question is, where the heck are Bobby Kay and his companions now?"

I scanned the room for anything helpful, while Al looked through the rest of the papers on the desk. I pressed a key on Bobby's laptop.

"Can we get access to this?"

Al nodded. "It might take a while, though."

"Knock yourself out," I said and moved to the side.

Reese looked up at me, her eyes darkened by sadness. "But wait. If they're out there and going to start a war, then where is Abby?"

"She must be with them," I said. "They probably took her with them."

"But what are they going to do with her? And where did they go? Where did they take my baby?" she asked, tears welling up in her eyes. "Will I ever see her again? Where is she, Harry?"

"I think I might be able to answer that," Al said.

She was staring at the screen in front of her. I walked up behind her and saw the screensaver photo on the laptop. It showed Candice and Bobby Kay in front of what looked like the entrance to a bunker. He had his arm around her, and they were smiling widely at the camera, looking happy.

Al tapped on the screen with her gloved finger.

"My guess is this is where they went to prepare for the next phase."

"A bunker?"

She nodded. "That's where I'd hide out when things got ugly."

"But, where is that bunker?" I asked. "How do we find it?"

"You're in luck. I happen to know exactly where that is," Al said, breathing heavily behind the gasmask. She rose to her feet and looked at me. I could barely see her eyes inside of that thing. She reminded me mostly of a giant mosquito.

"I'll take you there."

Chapter 38

REESE CLOSED her eyes inside the car. Her head was spinning, and she couldn't get a moment of rest from it. The voices were back, and they were all talking at once. Her brain was racing and wouldn't stop. She just wanted it, for once, to be nice and quiet and silent. She was on her medication, and that subdued them slightly, but lately, they wouldn't leave her alone. It was like they had all these messages they were trying to get through to her all at once.

Like they were trying to tell her something.

It had started when she was seventeen, a few months after she had been raped. That was the first time she remembered hearing the voices, and right after that, she had started believing her mother was trying to kill her. She had been obsessed with the thought that she wanted to hurt her, especially when she talked about taking her to see a therapist. So, once she was off to college, she believed she was finally free, that the voices would leave her alone, now that there was nothing to fear. But then she started having the same thoughts about her roommate, thinking she wanted to kill her, and that's when she realized something was terribly wrong. She was first diagnosed with bipolar disorder, but she knew that wasn't it. It wasn't right. Two years later, she was finally diagnosed with schizophrenia and put on the medication that had helped her ever since. There were good days and bad days. Today was one of the bad ones. There had been many times she had gone off her medicine for different reasons, and every time, it made her lose the memories of what she had done. All that was left were these images, these dreamlike pictures in her head that she didn't know if they were true or not. They all felt like when she believed her mother would kill her. The feeling of being betrayed or of someone being after you was so real, yet she couldn't tell if it really was. For the most part, it was just illusions in her mind, and sometimes even hallucinations. So, what could she trust?

"Are you all right back there?" Harry asked, looking at her in the rearview mirror. She was hugging herself bending forward, eyes closed.

Now, she opened them and looked at him.

"I think so."

They were driving out of town. Harry got them through the roadblock using his badge, telling the officers he was out on police business.

No one asked any questions. They all had that terrified look on their faces behind the masks, scared of being infected.

Reese could hear Abby now as they drove through the swampy landscape and hugged herself tighter when something else entered her mind, and her eyes shot open at once. She went over it in her mind, again and again.

Oh, God, let me remember.

She bit her lip. A flicker of pain followed, *no don't get upset...that won't help. For God's sake, think.*

Was it a memory? Could she trust it? Or was it just in her head?

No, this is real. This is very real, Reese.

Harry drove up a gravel road between the tall trees, then headed through marshland before entering a small forest-like area with heavy Spanish moss dangling from the trees. Wild Florida nature was growing everywhere, obviously having been left out of human touch for a very long time. Yet, there was still a trail for the car, and that told her there had been other cars here recently. Soon, in the distance, what looked like an abandoned building showed up as if out of nowhere. It seemed strange to see a concrete structure in the middle of all this wildlife that appeared to have once been an orange grove.

Harry stopped the car and killed the engine.

"The entrance is inside," Al said and pointed.

"Harry?" Reese said and looked out the window. "Harry? I need to talk to you."

Harry got out of the car, then pulled out his gun. Al followed him, also pulling out a weapon and cocking it. The sight of the guns made Reese wince.

"Not now, Reese. We can talk later," he said. "Stay here in the car."

"No, Harry. I think I need to tell you something," she said, but he had already slammed the door shut behind him and had started walking up toward the entrance of the building.

Inside the car, Reese whispered to herself:

"I think it might be important."

Chapter 39

"I USED to study places like these. It was a hobby of mine. I visited bomb shelters all over the country, including this one. It's been a few years, though."

Al was leading the way, showing me inside a small concrete building not much bigger than a shed in the middle of nowhere. We used our phones as flashlights to get down the many concrete stairs leading to the basement six feet underground. There were rusty metal beams on the floor, and I found an old wall calendar from the sixties. Al guided me down a concrete hallway and stopped in front of a huge steel door.

"This bunker was originally built as a protective shelter for survivors of a nuclear war," she said. "Now, most people don't even know it exists. It was built back in the nineteen-sixties, at the height of the cold war and often referred to as the Miami Catacombs. It's supposedly a five-thousand-square-foot maze of chambers and tunnels. Entering the shelter was a one-way trip. Its two-thousand-pound steel door was meant to seal survivors inside perma-nently. Once the door was shut, it couldn't be opened from the inside. The inhabitants were meant to get out of the catacombs by digging out using tunnels that had been partly pre-excavated. They would then have radiation-free seeds with them to take to the surface that they could sow in the earth and start life all over."

"Who was supposed to use this?" I asked and looked at the two-thousand-pound steel door in front of us. It was massive.

"It's actually privately owned, except no one cares about it now. Too expensive, I guess, too much upkeep. But it was built and paid for by one hundred individuals from twenty-five of Miami's wealthiest families."

"Of course," I said and touched the outside of the door with a scoff. "Gotta save those rich people so they can repopulate the earth."

Al sent me a look.

"It's said they even built a room designated to hold corpses, should any of them die while they were inside the shelter. Today, it's left completely abandoned."

She shone her flashlight across the dirty ground and up the sides of the massive green door. It was left open, and we walked right in. We ended up in a stairwell, which led to a four-inch wooden door that opened into the shelter itself. Al opened it carefully, and we walked inside, cautious not to make a sound.

The air was humid already after a few steps inside. It smelled old and musty inside the first room.

"This is the decontamination area," Al whispered. "Supposed to be used by anyone coming in that might have been contaminated by radioactive fallout."

It was hard to tell that this rusty old dirty place had ever been anything but abandoned. We continued through another wooden door that led us into what might have been a recreational area or meeting room of some sort, judging from the rusty furniture—what might have been a couch at some point, and shelves, and a lamp that had completely fallen apart. I found a puzzle that was so moldy you couldn't see what it was supposed to be on the picture. Under the ceiling hung droplets of water, and the paint had fallen off in big patches. The room ended in several hallways, leading left and right.

"Where do we go now?" I asked Al.

If this was a maze, then we risked getting lost in here. She shone her flashlight down one hallway, then another. She stood very still for a long time, listening, and I with her. Then she turned to gaze up at me from behind her mosquito mask. She signaled for me to be quiet and follow her, so I did.

Chapter 40

"CANDICE? I'm so sorry...for all this."

Candice growled behind the gag. She was breathing heavily in agitation while the person sitting next to her spoke, fear racing through her chest, constricting it, making it hard to breathe properly.

"It was never meant to end like this," he continued. "I hope you know this. I'm telling you the truth."

I hope you know this? It was never meant to end like this? How else was it supposed to end, huh? Explain that to me!

She wanted to yell at him for being such a fool, for using her the way he had. And now, he had the audacity to sit there and apologize? As if sorry would help him in any way.

It's too late, buddy. The ship has sailed. People are dying. And you want to apologize? You want my forgiveness? Is that it?

She shook her head, grunting behind the gag.

"I know, I know," he said, sounding melancholic. "I've been an idiot. I used you. You probably know this by now, but I was the one who took that virus from your lab. I stole the keycard from your purse one day when visiting and went that same night. We broke into your lab and stole it. I knew all your codes, and frankly, it was a little too easy. We covered our tracks well. You didn't even suspect a thing. You didn't even see that one of the samples was gone, did you? I thought that would be the hard part, but it wasn't. I don't know what I was thinking, going through with this. I thought you'd never have to know. Gosh, I was a fool."

Yes, you were a fool. No, that's not even enough. You were a complete idiot! Releasing a deadly virus into the population—how could you have been so stupid? How could anyone be so moronic? You think you can make amends now? By bringing me here and saying you're sorry?

Candice wanted so badly to say these things, to yell them at him, but she couldn't. All that left her mouth was growls and grunts. She felt a deep stab of pain in her jaw as she tried to move it. It had been locked in that same position for too long; it was beginning to hurt terribly.

"So, what was the plan by doing it, you might ask," he said with a deep sigh. "I wish I could answer that. It has all gone completely awry."

Candice tried to calm herself. It wasn't good to get too agitated behind the gag. She began so easily to hyperventilate, and that only made things worse. Often, she had trouble breathing, and she'd gasp for air.

"As I said, I'm terribly sor…"

He stopped himself. It took Candice a few seconds before she realized why he had paused mid-sentence. But as she stopped breathing so heavily, she heard it too.

There were steps outside the door—footsteps sounding very different from the ones she was used to hearing when she was brought food and water. They stopped by the door, and that was when her heart dropped.

"Did you hear that?" he asked.

She nodded, wondering who could be out there.

Bobby moved around next to her, and then started to yell:

"In here! We're in here! Help!"

Hearing him scream that made Candice's pulse quicken. Why was he calling for help? Wasn't he the one keeping her here? And why would he call for them to come inside, risking cutting the wire and setting off the bomb?

Didn't he know about the bomb?

Don't! Bobby, don't!

But, of course, he couldn't hear her behind the gag, and he continued.

"In here! Help! HELP!"

Chapter 41

REESE FELT UNEASY. It was like her head was about to explode. She couldn't sit still inside the car and had to get out. When it finally became too much for her, she opened the door and stepped out.

"I have to talk to Harry," she mumbled, anxiously walking back and forth, her toes in the flipflops getting dirty from the dust that she whirled up. "I have to tell him what I remember. He has to know."

No, Reese. He told you to wait.

Reese glared toward the small shed-like concrete building, biting her nails, calming herself, telling herself it could wait. She could tell Harry everything once he got back. She took a deep breath, and her shoulders came down slightly. She exhaled again, and just as she let the air back out, she was certain she heard something. Something that just about stopped her heart from beating: her eyes grew wide, and, without blinking, she looked toward the small building where Al and Harry had disappeared.

Was it a baby she could hear? Was it a baby crying, and was the sound coming from inside that place?

Reese gasped and clasped her chest, barely able to breathe. Never had she heard it so vividly. Never had she felt her daughter's presence so clearly.

My baby! It is her. I can hear her crying. She's here.

Her heart knocking against her ribcage, Reese stared at the door. They had left it ajar, and she could peek inside and see the stairs leading down. She wondered if she should just go in.

No, Reese. Harry told you to stay where you were. For once, do as you're told. He'll yell at you if you don't listen. You know he will. He wants to protect you. It might get dangerous down there.

Reese turned her back on the shed and walked to the car, determined to ignore the crying. It was probably only in her head anyway—just like all the other times when she felt certain she had heard Abby crying. She placed her hand on the handle and was about to open the car door when she hesitated.

What if it really was her baby down there? What if Abby was in there somewhere? She could be in danger.

I can't just wait here while my baby...while my child...I have to get her. She's crying for me.

Reese let go of the door handle, then took a few steps toward the shed when she changed her mind once again and paused at the entrance. She looked inside at the concrete stairs leading six feet down. Her hand on the door was shaking heavily as her baby's crying intensified. She closed her eyes and shook her head.

How could she ignore it? How could she not go?

Reese's eyelids shot open, and she stared into the deep darkness, then made her final decision. She pulled the door fully open, then walked in, whispering anxiously under her breath as she reached the stairs leading down, the crying becoming so loud she could barely hear her own thoughts:

"Mommy is coming, Abby. Mommy is coming now."

Chapter 42

AL STOPPED MIDWAY down a long hallway by a steel door. We had been through so many rooms that had just been left there, with bunk beds, desks, and even books on the shelves, for sixty years. It was all covered in mold, and the bunk beds were rusty, and the mattresses beyond disgusting. The air was thick and musty. It felt damp and clammy against my skin.

"Why are you stopping?" I asked.

Al raised a hand.

"Shh, listen. Did you hear that?"

"Hear what?"

She signaled for me to be quiet, so I shut up. I heard a small voice, yelling for help. It was coming from behind the steel door in front of us.

"HELP."

Al turned to look up at me. There was deep concern in her voice.

"Someone is behind that door."

"We're in here! Help!"

I looked at Al, then at the door, wondering who it

could be. If it was Bobby Kay and his group, then why were they calling for help? It sounded like a man's voice, so it couldn't be Candice, could it?

"What do we do?" Al asked.

With the gun in my hand, I walked to the door and knocked on it. The sound of my voice echoed in the empty hallways.

"Who is in there?"

A second passed before the voice answered. "Our names are Candice and Bobby Kay Smith. We're being held against our will in here. Please, get us out."

I exchanged a look with Al, then didn't think about it twice. I grabbed the door handle and pushed it down.

"It's open," I said and glanced happily at Al.

I was about to push it fully open and storm inside when Al stopped me, putting a hand on my arm. She shook her head.

"If they're being kept against their will, wouldn't the door be locked?" she asked. "Why was it left open?"

"What are you saying?"

"Something is wrong," she said.

I pulled the door closed again. "What do you mean? Like what?"

"Here, let me," she said, then knelt by the door. She grabbed the handle and opened it cautiously, pushing it open only a hairsbreadth. Then she slid a gloved hand inside slowly till it touched something, and she pulled it back immediately. Fearful eyes glared up at me.

"There's a wire. It's a bomb, Harry. If you push that door open, we'll all die."

I held my breath. I had been less than a second from doing just that. My hands started shaking at the mere thought. I could have killed us all by acting hastily.

"Dear God," I said. "What do we do?"

Al nodded. "I might know how to disable something like that. I felt it gently. It seems like straightforward construction—something anyone could do."

"Have you done something like this before?" I asked.

She nodded. "I've done it quite a few times, yes."

"Why doesn't that surprise me?" I said, feeling slightly relieved.

Al sent me a smile from behind the mask, then knelt by the door again and reached inside. I held my breath as she fumbled with the wire, praying under my breath that the bomb wouldn't suddenly go off.

I didn't even see Reese storm toward us until it was too late. All I heard was her screaming something about her baby being in there, about her baby crying for her, and then she yelled: *Mommy is coming*, before she pushed the door open and burst right into the wire, jerking it.

Chapter 43

EVERYTHING STOPPED. At first, I wasn't blinking; I wasn't even thinking. I just stood there, staring at my sister as she burst into the room.

NO!

I waited for the explosion. I expected it, telling myself this was it, closing my eyes, and preparing myself for the blast throwing me up in the air and ripping us all to pieces.

But it didn't happen.

For some reason, it didn't go off.

I looked down at Al, who was sitting by the doorstep, holding a small device in her hand. She wasn't breathing either.

"I managed to take the wire out just at the instant she came through," she stuttered after a few seconds of regaining her composure.

Meanwhile, Reese was inside the room, screaming her baby's name.

"Abby? Abby? Where are you, sweetie? Mommy is here. I'm here."

But there was no baby anywhere. Only two people

sitting on a mattress, their arms and legs tied up. One was also blindfolded and gagged. I guessed that had to be Candice. The other I recognized as Bobby Kay. He didn't look like he knew about the bomb, and he stared at me, eyes wide open.

"Was that…a…"

Al nodded. She pointed at the backpack next to the door, then peeked inside. "Just as I thought. Full of explosives."

Bobby Kay's nostrils were flaring aggressively, and he had a vein popping out on his forehead.

"You mean to say we almost…she almost…you… you…oh, dear God."

I knelt in front of Candice and grabbed her hands in mine while I spoke to her calmly.

"Hello, Candice. My name is Detective Harry Hunter. I've been looking for you. I'm going to release you now. I'll try my best not to hurt you."

I leaned over and took off the blindfold first. Candice blinked her eyes and narrowed them as the bright florescent light from inside the room hit them and blinded her momentarily.

"Keep them closed for a few seconds until they get used to the light," I told her, then moved on to the cloth covering her mouth. I untied it, then pulled it out. She gagged a few times, then coughed and leaned forward, moving her jaw. It looked painful. Her eyes finally opened and landed on me. Then, she tried to smile.

"Thank you," she whispered.

I untied her feet and arms as well, and I could tell it hurt to move them, but she was greatly relieved finally to be free.

"How about me?" Bobby Kay said and lifted his tied hands. "Aren't you going to free me?"

While Candice tried to get to her feet, I approached him. I knelt in front of him, looking him straight in the eyes.

"You and I need to have a chat first," I said. "You've got a lot of explaining to do before I trust you enough to let you go."

Bobby Kay sighed and leaned against the wall behind him. "Fair enough. What do you want to know?"

I was about to speak when Reese moved in front of me. She was almost screaming at him.

"First of all, tell me...where is my baby? What did you do to Abby?"

Bobby Kay looked at her, puzzled.

"You don't remember, Reese?"

Chapter 44

REESE STOOD like she was frozen. Her heart hammered in her chest, and she couldn't think straight. She had heard her baby crying as she ran down the hallways of the bunker, stumbling through room after room of dirty old rusty, moldy furniture, searching for her when she had been certain she heard her behind the steel door. Thinking she had no time to waste, she had sprung through it, bursting inside, desperately searching for her poor child, but the moment she stepped inside, it had stopped. The crying had ceased just as suddenly as it had begun. Now, she was standing in front of Bobby Kay, who was sitting on the mattress, tied up. She looked into his eyes as he said the words.

Don't you remember?

"Remember what?"

Bobby Kay scoffed. "You really don't, do you? You don't recall that the DCF took her? They came to your apartment one day and took her from you. They put her in foster care because you couldn't take care of her properly. Because of your condition, they said, because you had gone off your meds. We tried to help you through our foundation. That's how we met. I saw you crying at the CVS where you work. I stop by there when I need a new inhaler, around once a month. That day, I saw you crying behind the building and walked around it to talk to you. You told me what had happened, how they had taken your child, and you didn't know what to do next. On that day, I promised to help you. It wasn't unusual for me. We do stuff like that from time to time for people, you know, for the little people in society who can't pay for a lawyer on their own. Those that have met injustice in the system and need help. I had my lawyers look at your case, and they believe that you have a case and that they can help you. In fact, until this virus happened, they were still working to win back your baby. You're telling me you really don't remember?"

Reese stared at the man in front of her as she realized she did remember. As he told her these things, she now saw the faces of the people taking her baby. She vaguely remembered the woman from DCF who had come to her apartment on several occasions, talking to her, observing her with the baby.

"Is this true, Reese?" Harry asked. He turned to face her. "Reese?"

Tears welled up in her eyes as she thought about that day when they had knocked on her door. The more she thought about that day, the more the blanks were being filled in, and the more it now made sense. Her baby had been crying day and night, and Reese hadn't known what to do. She had refused to go back on her meds when they asked. She argued that she felt fine, yet the voices and hallucinations had grown terribly strong and made her incapable of taking care of the poor crying baby. The lack of sleep hadn't exactly helped her situation either.

That's why I keep hearing her cry. I didn't take care of her properly. I wasn't good enough.

"Reese?"

She looked up at her brother, then felt the tears escape her eyes even though she tried to stifle them. Then, she nodded.

"So, it's true?" Harry asked. "DCF took your baby, not the foundation? Not Bobby Kay and his people?"

Reese nodded. "Yes. I...I think I remember now."

Harry scoffed, then turned to face Bobby Kay again. "And what was in it for you? What was your price for helping my sister? That she got infected with the virus and went into society to spread it so you could create a New World Order, or what the heck it was you were planning? Did you use Reese's situation to pressure her into helping you? You needed someone like her, am I right? How else would you spread the deadly virus that you stole from your sister?"

Chapter 45

"NO."

I clenched my fist. I had to tread carefully now, not act out in agitation. The thought of my sister being used this way was making my blood boil.

"What do you mean, *no*?" I asked and eased the tension in my shoulders slightly. I held my hand on the grip of the gun that had gone back in its holster when untying Candice.

"No, that was not my intention at all. To use Reese," Bobby Kay said.

I narrowed my eyes. "I don't believe you."

"But it's the truth, nonetheless," he said. "I'm not proud of what happened at all. This was never my intention. I had different plans for the virus."

"Really? Like what?" Al asked from behind me. "Why did you take the virus?"

Bobby Kay sighed. His shoulders slumped. Candice, his sister, was staring at him. We were all waiting for answers.

"It wasn't really my idea at all," he said. "But one day, we were hanging out at the house, talking about the future for our group, when I accidentally mentioned my sister's work. There isn't a minute that I don't regret having told them about it. Jacob and Petra both got that weird look in their eyes and started having all these strange ideas about us stealing the virus, and then we'd have a weapon. We could use it to press the politicians into meeting our demands. I don't know if you heard about David Brunner?"

"Sure," Al said. "He was imprisoned because he published undisclosed documents on WikiLeaks. Civil rights organizations argue that what he did shouldn't be punishable because his activity mirrors conduct that investigative journalists regularly undertake in their professional capacity. Prosecuting David Brunner could cause journalists to self-censor out of fear of prosecution as well, which would be bad for our constitutional rights of freedom of expression."

"Exactly," Bobby Kay said. "We've been running a campaign for his release and tried to influence government officials into helping us plead for his release, but we were getting nowhere. No one was listening to us. Somehow, Jacob and Petra got it in their heads that with this virus, threatening to release it, they would comply. I told them those were the methods of terrorists, and we'd end up being listed as such, as a terrorist organization, but they wouldn't listen. They're the money behind this entire foundation; if they pull out, we're left with nothing, so as they pushed for me to get ahold of the virus, I finally complied. I visited Candice and took her keycard, then broke into the lab and took a sample of the virus. I thought I'd be able to take it back once our demands were met and Brunner released. I thought no one would ever have to know. I honestly thought I was helping a humanitarian cause. I was an idiot."

"You think?" I asked.

I felt Al's hand on my arm. She was telling me to back off.

"But then what happened?" she asked. "How did the virus end up in Reese, and how did you end up down here?"

"They turned on me and our original plan. The others went behind my back and injected Reese with the virus. They never even told me they had done it. I merely realized the sample was gone. But I had my suspicions, and that's why I started following her and later mapping her whereabouts to see if there was a pattern for where she had been and clusters of infections. Seeing her state of mind, how she was very obviously sick and running a fever, confirmed my suspicion. I even went to her workplace and asked her if she was all right. But she just said she was fine. She had a sore throat; that was all. For a long time, I told myself it wasn't the virus, that she just had the flu or a bad cold, that I was being paranoid. Still, I couldn't look away from the fact that everywhere she had been, there were new clusters, lots of infected people. By the time I finally admitted it to myself, it was too late. She had already infected hundreds of people, and it didn't take long before all hell broke loose. I watched, terrified, as it was all over the news. I asked the others about it, about what had happened to the virus. No one wanted to admit they had done it. I got scared and didn't know what to do. Later, I told the others that I wanted to come clean. We had to tell the authorities what they were dealing with, what we had done, that we had taken the virus and somehow it had been set free in the public. I was scared, especially once you came knocking on our door. I didn't know they had already taken Candice. I hadn't spoken to her in weeks since I was so terrified that she'd figure out it was me who took it. But when you told me she was gone, I suspected the others had kidnapped her so she wouldn't tell anyone what they had done—so she wouldn't be able to tell that they had released a genetically created virus and caused the entire world to go into lockdown. I pretended that I didn't know her very well, so you'd leave, then I confronted them, and they knocked me down. I woke up down here with my sister. I didn't even see them put the wire on the bomb. I had no idea that it was there."

"And the baby? Why was there a baby at your place when I was there?" I asked. "If it wasn't Reese's baby?"

He looked confused, then shrugged. "That could have been Loretta's. She's my cleaning lady. She recently had a baby, and she brings it to work. She doesn't have anyone to take care of the child while she works. It doesn't bother me that she brings him."

"So, you're telling us that you had nothing to do with Reese being infected at all? That you didn't even know about it? How are we supposed to believe that? You're the leader of OUTRAGED, aren't you? How could you not know what was happening?"

"I don't know how to make you believe what I'm saying," he said. "They don't tell me everything. I'm just the spokesman, the front figure if you will because of my fame. They're the ones making the decisions, not me."

I shook my head. "I don't believe you."

Reese approached me. Her big eyes lingered on me.

"He's telling the truth, Harry. That was what I was about to tell you earlier. While we drove here, it came back to me. I remembered something. I tried to tell you, but you didn't have time to listen."

My eyes met hers. She wasn't really there as she was

pondering something, trying to make sense of her thoughts.

"What, Reese? What did you remember?"

Her eyes came back to me, and she gave me a faint smile.

"I think I remember who gave me the injection."

"And it wasn't Bobby Kay?" I asked, puzzled.

She shook her head.

"No."

"And this isn't just one of your hallucinations or voices telling you this?" I asked, concerned.

"Not this time. This is what really happened. The memory is crystal clear in my mind."

I was waiting anxiously for her reply when my phone suddenly vibrated in my pocket, and I pulled it out.

"It's Jean," I said and picked it up. "I have to take it."

"Harry?" she said on the other end. I didn't like the tone of her voice. She was crying. "Oh, Harry, honey."

"What? What's going on, Jean? Is it Josie? Did something happen to Josie? Jean?"

Chapter 46

*HER CONDITION GOT WORSE the past few hours, and they
have to intubate her now. The doctor says he's not sure her heart can
take it. I'm so sorry, Harry. I'm so terribly sorry.*

Jean's words rang in my mind as I rushed back toward
town. Everyone was in the car with me—Al, Reese,
Candice, and Bobby Kay. I had no plan. I didn't even have
an idea of a plan, not even a sketch. I hadn't even thought
about what to do next. I just knew I had to get back to
town to get to my daughter.

A thunderstorm had pulled in over town, and as we got
closer, the dark clouds surrounded us above our heads, and
a few seconds later, the heavy rain poured down on us. I
barely noticed. All I could think about was my daughter,
my poor baby girl.

I had called my dad from the car to check in on him,
and he sounded weak but said he was okay. He had taken
his temperature just a few minutes before I called, and it
was down from this morning, which was the first sign of
progress I had seen in him so far. I told him about Josie,

crying my heart out in despair, and he went completely quiet on the other end. I hadn't realized until now that he naturally blamed himself for having infected Josie.

"I brought this to her," he suddenly said. "I brought it into your house, and now she's fighting for her life because of me."

"No, Dad. You can't think like that, you hear me? I might as well have been the one to bring it into our house and infect you and her. We can never know for sure where it came from."

"Don't patronize me, son," he said. "I know I was the one. You never had any symptoms."

"Some people don't get any," I said. "Some are just asymptomatic carriers. I connect with many people in my daily work. I'm telling you; it might as well have been me."

He didn't believe me. Of course, he didn't. If I didn't believe myself, how could he believe me? We both knew I was just talking to make him feel better about himself. I didn't want him to blame himself. But the fact was, there were times I'd think that maybe this wouldn't have happened if I hadn't asked him to move in with us, to be with Josie while I was at work. Perhaps she could have been spared that way. I guess I blamed both of us, but mostly myself.

I stopped the car in front of Jackson Memorial and got out without saying anything to the passengers in my car. I didn't know if I should arrest Bobby Kay or not. He'd have to answer for his actions of stealing the virus; that was for sure. But he had told me he'd come willingly to the station and explain everything. He needed to get it off his chest. He couldn't live like this anymore.

But all of that had to wait. Right now, I could only focus on my daughter. My poor, poor girl who was being intubated, who was struggling to do something as simple as breathe—whose heart was failing her once again.

Please, don't take her from me, God. I don't know where you are in all this; I can't feel you anywhere. But, please, I beg you. Let me keep her.

I ran to the sliding doors when a guard came up toward me, wearing a shield in front of his face, a stern look in his eyes behind the clear plastic.

"Sir, I'm gonna have to stop you right here."

"Please," I said. "You don't understand. My daughter…she's just…she's being intubated right now. At least let me see her one last time in case she doesn't make it. She must be so scared right now. I need to be with her, please."

He shook his head. "I'm sorry, sir. There's nothing I can do. If she worsens, the nurses will Facetime you so you can say goodbye. But for now, I need you to step outside the hospital grounds. Those are the rules. No visitors."

Tears ran across my cheeks so fast I couldn't wipe them away fast enough. "Facetime me? They'll Facetime me to say goodbye to my daughter? What? How…how can you…how can they do this?"

The guard sighed deeply. He, too, had tears in his eyes that he was struggling to hide.

"I'm sorry, sir. You're not the first parent I had to stop today. It's the same for everyone. I can't let you in."

I stepped outside, then fell to my knees in the rain, tears springing from my eyes.

Someone has to pay. Someone must pay for this!

I lifted my gaze toward the crying sky above me, feeling a fire rise inside me, a burning desire to do something, anything.

"This ends here," I said into the rain. "I'm ending it now."

Reese came out of the car and ran to me. She put her arm around me and helped me get up. I grabbed her by the shoulders and forced her to look straight at me.

"I need you to tell me everything."

Chapter 47

THE THREE-STORY MANSION seemed deserted from the outside, but a car in the driveway told me we might be in luck. I drove my car up in front of it, then parked. I looked in the rearview mirror as my three colleagues parked their cars on the street, blocking it so no one could leave the property in case they tried to run.

I had dropped Bobby Kay and Candice off at the station and told Major Walker to have someone take their statements, then added that he might want to call the FBI and alert their Joint Terrorism Task Force since we were dealing with domestic terrorism. After listening to him reprimand me for breaking my quarantine, I told him everything in brief sentences. When he was done listening and had heard the story, he contacted the Florida Chief Justice. It felt like forever while they spoke on the phone. Finally, he returned to me, holding the arrest warrant.

"Please, don't let me down on this one, Hunter. I've put my entire reputation on the line here. Yours too."

He handed the warrant to me and gave me three colleagues to bring with me. Hands on the grips of our guns, we walked up to the front door while I left Al and Reese in the car.

"Police! Open up."

When nothing happened, I kicked in the door. It swung open, and we went in, my three colleagues going in before me, clearing the way. Officer Fox, or Foxy, as we called him, grabbed the door handle leading to the living room and stepped inside. As he did, six shots were fired at him.

Pop-pop-pop-pop-pop-pop.

The sound was overpowering. Foxy's body jerked and went into spasms before falling to the ground with a thud. The rest of us came crashing down behind his dead body, the wind being blown out of my lungs. I managed to turn over a table so it could be used as protection as more shots were fired at us, bullets flying around our ears. The shots continued, and the bullets were screaming past us.

We shot back relentlessly. But theirs didn't die down. They kept going at it like they had an endless supply of bullets. I exchanged a look with the officer to my left, Officer Hanson, and signaled for him to cover me. I was going to try and get closer to be able to see inside the living room. He fired a round of shots, and theirs died down for a second, just enough for me to crawl forward on my hands and knees, heading for the door. Never had five feet seemed so far away.

More shorts followed as Hanson stopped to reload. I laid down flat on the floor when a shot hit a full-sized mirror behind me, and it exploded, raining pieces of glass down on all of us. I closed my eyes and let them fall, then felt a stabbing pain in the back of my leg as a piece of the mirror went through it. Behind me, Officer Hanson screamed as his shooting hand had been cut by a big piece of mirror, and blood was gushing out.

I pulled the piece of glass out of my leg with a growl,

then ripped a piece of my shirt off and tied it around the wound to stop the bleeding. With throbbing pain in the back of my lower leg, I wormed forward until I reached the doorframe. I pulled myself up so I could look inside, only the top of my hair being in the open. I peeked inside, moving swiftly.

The first thing I saw was the pool of blood on the floor. The adrenaline was clamping my throat as I stared at the two bodies.

Wincing in pain from my leg, I managed to get up on my knees, get my gun ready, then stuck my arm inside and fired a round of shots in the direction where the bullets were coming from.

There was a thud, then a bump, and then nothing.

Inside the living room, everything had suddenly gone quiet.

Chapter 48

HAD I HIT THE SHOOTER? Was that what this sudden silence meant? Or was it a trick to lure me out in the open? To get me to walk in and then finish me off?

I turned to look at Officer Hanson; he was okay. He was in obvious pain but breathing. Breathing was good. But he couldn't shoot anymore. I then turned to my last helping hand, Officer Conley. He was a big guy and not fast on his feet. He wouldn't be able to move quickly if this turned out to be a trick.

I decided to test it. I grabbed one of my shoes, then pulled it off and threw it through the door opening. It landed inside on the floor with a bump, but nothing else happened. I waited a few more seconds, just to be sure, then decided it was enough.

I rose to my feet, then went for it. I rushed inside, pointed my gun in the direction of the shooter, but as I did, I saw nothing. No one was there.

Not even the shooter's dead body.

"Shooter is gone," I yelled, then took off. The only way out was the big sliding doors leading to the massive backyard and the water behind it. If there was a boat at the dock, the shooter might escape that way.

I stormed to the end of the living room and out the open sliding doors. My eyes scanned the area outside, but I didn't see anything at first. The pool area, the tennis courts…everything was empty. Then, I spotted something —a figure darting across the grass and down the yard toward the water.

I took off, sprinting in the same direction. The figure had gotten a pretty good head start, though, and I would have to push myself to catch up. I had long legs and was a good runner, and soon I was storming down the grass toward the water. My joints were aching, and my muscles felt like they were burning. I was going fast, but the figure was too far ahead of me. If there were a boat by the docks or another outlet, I wouldn't be able to get there in time. I assumed there had to be some way out by the end of the lot; otherwise, the shooter wouldn't try to get out this way. I tried to push myself harder but wasn't gaining anything. The yard felt endless, and I was about to give up reaching there in time when I saw something come out between the trees at the bottom of the yard, running directly toward the shooter. It took me a few seconds to see what it was and realize it was a person. This person leaped for the figure at the bottom of the yard, arms reaching out. The person crashed on top of the shooter, causing the body to tumble into the grass.

As I got closer, I realized this someone was wearing a full-body hazmat suit and a gasmask.

It looked mostly like a giant mosquito in full-blown attack-mode.

Chapter 49

AL!

They were fighting in the grass. The shooter was trying to get loose from Al's grip. But she was quite the fighter, despite her small size. She knew quite a few tricks, and soon, the shooter was pinned to the ground, her on top of him.

I approached them, panting agitatedly.

"Al! What the heck? Where did you come from?"

"I heard the shots and got out of the car to see what was happening…to make sure you were all right. That's when I saw him run out the doors. I stole a golf cart that was parked by the tennis courts and drove till I reached the trees where I couldn't get any closer, then ran the rest of the way."

I smiled while catching my breath and leaning on my knees.

"You're amazing; do you know that?"

"I do," she said. She looked down at James Hudson beneath her, struggling to get up, but having no luck. "You done?"

He became quiet. I pointed my gun at him.

"You can let go now," I said to Al. "I got him."

"It's okay," she said. "I kind of enjoy sitting on him, holding him down. I could give him another round if you like. Ruffle him up a bit."

"It's okay," I said and reached down to pick up James's gun from the grass, where he had dropped it when Al attacked him. "I have a feeling this is between him and me right now."

Al crawled off him, and he sat up, dusting grass off his clothes.

"How so?" Al asked. "How is it between you and him?"

"Well, at first, I yielded mostly to your theory," I said. "That it was all some attempt to change the world we live in, but as soon as Reese told me the name of the guy that had injected her with the virus, that it was James Hudson here, I suddenly remembered where I had heard his name before. And that was when I realized this was personal. I thought he had chosen Reese because she was an easy target. After all, she was off her meds and had no idea what she was doing...or they thought they could get her to do anything for them since they promised to help her get her kid back, but that wasn't why at all. He had chosen Reese because he wanted to kill her. And not just that, he wanted to kill my family and me as well. This was never about infecting the entire world; it was all about my family and me. That's why he gave Reese the virus. She told me he came to her apartment and attacked her. He knocked her out before he injected the virus in her blood. That's why she didn't remember it until now. She didn't know it had happened. When she woke up, he was gone, and she feared she had dreamt it or that it was a hallucination. She went about her day, went to work, and so on, infecting hundreds of people, and within days, the virus traveled all over the world, causing everything to shut down because so many got sick, especially children. She had no idea until she got very sick after five days and fainted at the supermarket. Four weeks in an induced coma and Jim here thought she was definitely dead. He had also thought she'd visit her family or that we'd at least see her in the hospital, somehow getting infected ourselves. When it didn't happen, and he realized I was searching for Candice, he hoped the bomb would take care of us. He wanted me to find her and Bobby. As a journalist, he is deemed an essential worker and can get through the roadblocks."

"But why, Harry? Why you?" Al asked.

I swallowed a growing knot in my throat when thinking about Josie and my dad. "Reese and I are the ones he wanted to hurt because Reese and I killed his mother."

"Excuse me?"

"Once I remembered his name, I realized this was what it was about. Revenge for his mother being killed when he was just a child. Reese had just gotten her driver's license a few months earlier, and we had taken a road trip to New York that weekend. Just the two of us. But while we were on the road, Reese lost control of the car and drove into the side of another car at an intersection. The driver of that car died instantly from the impact, while her little boy survived."

"And that little boy had nowhere to go after that," James Hudson said, looking up at us. "His dad didn't want him; his aunt wanted him but had no room, unfortunately. I was tossed into the system. The family that finally took me in changed their minds and left me at a fire station. I became angry and lashed out at everyone, then ended up growing up at an institution for troubled children. All because of you and your crazy sister. Because you were goofing around in the car, not paying attention to the road. You both got to go on with your lives, living with both your parents, while my life was destroyed forever."

As he said the last part, James pulled out a knife attached to his shin, then reached up and stabbed Al in the stomach. She gasped, then looked down at the gushing blood. James rose to his feet and tried to get away.

I screamed, lifted my gun, then fired it at James, shooting him in the upper part of his back, hitting him between the shoulder blades. He fell forward, face-first into the grass, and dropped the bloody knife.

Chapter 50

"HIS NAME IS JACOB LEBEDEV, and that over there is his sister, Petra Lebedev," I told the paramedics as they approached the two dead bodies inside the living room. It was almost evening now, and the sun was about to set. The place was crawling with people...police, paramedics, and techs. Keeping up the social distancing rules was turning out to be pretty difficult. Still, they were all doing their best. The paramedics had cleaned the wound on my leg and bandaged it, but it wasn't bleeding any more. Officer Hanson had been taken to the hospital for treatment of his hand, while Foxy had been taken away in a body bag.

Al had been airlifted in a chopper to the hospital, and another chopper had come to take James Hudson as well. I was hoping for his survival since I wanted him to have to be held responsible for what he had done to us all. I wanted the world to know what had really happened to us, and I wanted him punished for it for the rest of his life.

I just hoped the hospitals had the capacity to take care of two wounded people amid everything else that was going on.

"One heck of a mess, huh, Hunter?" my partner Propper said as he approached me yet stayed six feet away from me. He had been called in to help out since he hadn't shown any symptoms so far.

"How's the kid? How's Josie?"

I shook my head. I hadn't spoken to Jean in hours.

"I don't know."

Propper sent me a smile. "Guess the last thing you can do now is pray to that God of yours, huh?"

I smiled back. "It's never the *last* thing I do, Propper. Always the first. Besides, He'll come through for my family and me. Just you watch Him."

"I admire your faith; I must say that," Propper said. "Tell him, if He does, then I might even start coming to that church of yours."

"Careful what you say," I said. "I might hold you to your word."

Propper pointed at me with a grin when my phone rang in my pocket, and I pulled it out.

It was Jean.

"Harry, I'm sorry, but...I don't know how to tell you this. I am afraid she's gotten worse. Honey...I..."

My heart dropped instantly. I looked at Propper and thought about how I had just said all those things confidently, like I really believed them when the fact was that inside I was being ripped apart with worry. I had my faith, yes, but it was diminishing by the second, and right now, I was about to lose it.

"I'm sorry, Harry," Jean said. I could hear she was crying but fighting to keep it from me.

I hung up, wiping tears from my eyes, then looked around the room. Techs were working to secure evidence; the bodies were being taken away. There was no more use for me here, and there was somewhere I really needed to be right now.

Even if being there wouldn't make a difference.

Chapter 51

OF COURSE, my car broke down on the way there. I could see the hospital in the distance when the car suddenly died. I had asked Propper to drive Reese back to my house, before leaving. I turned it onto the side of the road, tried to get it back up and running, but the battery had died. It didn't even give me a cough. It was suddenly completely dead. I growled loudly, then walked out into the rain, pulling the collar of my Miami PD jacket up to cover my ears, closing it to keep the rain out, and decided to walk the rest of the way.

By the time I reached the hospital's entrance, I was completely soaked. Luckily, I wasn't cold since it was very hot out still. But my jeans had turned dark from the rain, and my hair was hanging flat, dripping on my face.

I sat down in the rain, back against the wall, staring at the entrance. I knew they wouldn't let me inside, no matter how much I begged, but this was the closest I could get to my daughter right now, so this was where I wanted to be. I didn't care about the rain soaking me or even the thunder I heard in the distance. I didn't care that it had gotten dark and night would come soon. This was the only place in the world that I wanted to be.

While sitting there, I texted my dad to check in on him. He didn't answer for quite some time, so I called instead. I was relieved once he picked up.

"Hello?"

"Dad, it's me. How are you doing?"

He groaned and wheezed into the phone. "Not good, son. Fever has gone up again tonight, and I'm struggling to breathe."

My heart dropped for the second time tonight, and I fought to keep my tears at bay.

"Where are you, son?"

A deep cough followed that turned into a fit of coughing, and for a second, I feared he would die on me right there. But he managed to get his breath back again.

"I'm outside the hospital, Dad. Josie's not doing so well. Do you want me to come home to you?"

"No," he said. "Don't you dare leave your post. Josie is the most important right now. I'm gonna be fine."

"I don't even know what I'm doing here," I sighed and glanced toward the closed doors. The security guard was standing right on the other side of them. "It's not like they'll let me see her; I just feel like this is where I should be, you know? I told Jean I was here. I keep thinking that if she's about to die, then they'll come to get me, right? I won't risk losing my chance at saying goodbye if there is one. I can't say goodbye to my daughter on Facetime. I simply refuse to."

"You won't have to. I'm sure you won't. God hasn't brought you this far to give up on you now."

"I'm not so sure anymore," I said. "I'm losing faith here, Dad. Why did Josie have to be infected in the first place? Why couldn't it have been me? She has a bad heart.

Why is God not removing all this? Why isn't He curing her if He allegedly loves me so much? I'm sorry, but I don't know if I can believe in Him coming through for me this time."

"So is His love for you based on what you see Him do for you?" my dad asked. "Is that how you can tell how much He loves you? You know that in this life you'll have trials; He never promised us life would be easy, that it would be a stroll in the park. But He does promise He'll get you through it."

"I'm not in the mood for this right now, Dad. The preaching. It's just not helping. And don't tell me that God has a plan for all of us, for Josie and me. I don't want to hear it. I'm angry at God right now, and there isn't anything you can say to change that."

"That's okay, son."

I hung up, feeling heavy-hearted. I sat in the rain, phone clenched between my hands, my stomach in knots. I wanted to pray at that moment, but somehow, I couldn't. I was so angry with God that the words remained locked in my throat. All I had were tears—tears streaming down my cheeks, while my head leaned against the wall behind me.

Chapter 52

AS I SAT THERE, soaked by the rain, eyes closed, I suddenly sensed that I wasn't alone. I opened my eyes and looked up at a man standing close to me with his arm stretched out toward me. I blinked a few times to better see his face in the scarce light from the lamps outside the hospital building.

"Old Man Jones?"

"I thought that was you, Detective."

He smiled. In his hand, he was holding a brown bag. He moved it toward me, and I took it, then looked inside.

It was a meatball sandwich.

"For you, my friend," he said and winked. "Looks like you need it more than I do."

"I can't take your food," I said.

"Too fancy to accept food from homeless people, Detective?" he said, lifting his eyebrows. "I won't take no for an answer."

I scoffed and sent him half a smile.

"Thank you. I appreciate it. Truly."

"Thought you might. Spending the night, are we?"

"I guess. My daughter's in there. I want to be as close to her as possible."

Old Man Jones chuckled, then whistled. Much to my surprise, he hadn't come alone. Behind him came out several other local homeless people. I knew their faces well from the streets and shelters. All of them came carrying things. One had a beat-up patio chair, another a big piece of cardboard and a blanket, while someone had brought me bottled water and a small bag of chips. All their gifts were carefully placed on the pavement in front of me.

"That should help you get through the night," Old Man Jones said. "The cardboard can shelter you from the rain if you put it up at an angle. You'll figure it out. You're after all a detective, right?"

"Right," I said, voice breaking, tears springing to my eyes. I couldn't believe these people would do all this for me. It was such a grand gesture; I had no words for it— none that would suffice.

"Thank you so much."

"No problem, Detective. We take care of one another in the streets; it doesn't matter where you come from," Old Man Jones said. He nodded in greeting, then turned on his heel and walked away without another word. His friends followed him into the night. I stared at them as they left, thinking about all the things I should have said and all the things I should have done to help these people, then wondered where they'd spend the night.

I placed the cardboard at an angle to block out the rain out made a part of it into a roof. I then sat in the old patio chair and ate the sandwich. I hadn't realized how hungry I was and gulped it down in a matter of minutes. I drank water greedily and ate the chips as well, then covered myself with the blanket and tried to get some sleep, listening to the rain drumming on my cardboard roof.

Chapter 53

I SLEPT SURPRISINGLY WELL despite the circumstances and woke up when someone called my name. As I opened my eyes, I realized the sun had risen, and it was already day. The rain had done what it came to do and left. I gasped, startled before I looked in the direction of the voice.

"Harry! Harry!"

It was Jean. She was rushing toward me, her shoes clacking on the pavement. She looked exhausted, which I assumed she was. I wondered if she even knew how many hours she had been working.

"Harry! I tried to call you; why didn't you pick up!"

I looked at my phone in my hand. It was dead.

"No more battery," I said, then realized that she was coming toward me, wearing no face covering at all. No mask, no protective shield, and she had taken off her suit. I stood to my feet, jolted upright, but before I could say anything, she jumped me and threw her arms around my neck.

She kissed me.

I pulled away, almost gasping.

"Wh…what are you doing?"

She looked at me, surprised. "Haven't you heard?"

"Haven't I heard what? I have been here all night, camped out, waiting for news about Josie."

"Harry. It's amazing. They found a cure for the Florida Flu. They found a treatment that really works. It's been through all the experimental testing and trials over the past few weeks, and the results were so good that the FDA has approved it. Some rich people in New York got together with a bunch of scientists and sponsored its development. And they moved fast. Tens of thousands of shipments were delivered all over the nation. We received a shipment of the treatment last night and started giving it to our worst-off patients. After less than ten hours of receiving this drug intravenously, they're all improving—all of them. They say that from now on, if you come down with this virus, if it's caught early on, then you'll just need a pill, and then it'll be over in a day. Isn't it wonderful?"

My heart was beating so fast now; it felt like it would explode. I grabbed Jean by the shoulders and looked into her eyes.

"I can't believe it. And Josie?"

"Just got taken off the ventilator. You can go see her now."

Jean didn't need to say that twice. I pulled off my mask that had been hanging around my neck, then threw it in the trash on my way inside, running past the security guard, who did nothing but smile and wave at me.

I ran to the elevator, Jean coming in behind me. She helped me find Josie on the third floor, where the atmosphere was more than amazing. Nurses were dancing, and doctors clapping as a long row of kids were rolled out into the hallway, leaving the ICU. The kids were smiling, and some were crying, others laughing.

Jean grabbed my hand and led me to a room, then opened the door. Inside, Josie was sitting in a bed. She was so pale, it was scary, but her eyes were alive and smiling.

"Dad!"

I ran to her, grabbed her in my arms, and hugged her so tight that I feared I might crush her fragile body.

"I can't believe it, Josie. You're better. You're better."

"The medicine worked, Dad."

"I got some for your father, too," Jean said and handed me a box of pills. "I spoke to a doctor about him a few minutes ago, and he said these would work. They are for patients who can still breathe on their own. It should do the trick for him. And I heard from a colleague earlier this morning that Al has come out of surgery, and she's going to make it. And so is James Hudson, even though he'll probably not walk again. It's the day of miracles."

I exhaled, satisfied, finally able to let go of the worry. Al was going to be fine; Hudson would be handed over to the FBI and was no longer my problem. Candice would get to go back to Bryan and meet him in real life, and hopefully, they'd like that just as much as dating through closed windows. The only thing that hadn't been solved was the story of Reese and her baby. I promised myself at that moment that I'd do all I could to help her in her fight to get her baby—and my niece—back.

I pulled Jean into a kiss.

"It sure is."

"Ew," Josie said when she saw us kiss. "Get a room, will you?"

That made me laugh, but then I paused.

"You know what? She's saying something."

Jean gave me a puzzled look.

"What exactly is she saying?"

"Maybe we should get a room together."

A frown grew between her eyebrows. "What are you talking about?"

I looked down at Jean and smiled. "How about we get married, and you come to live with us?"

That made Josie's face light up. "Oh, yes, that would be totally awesome. Please, say yes, Jean, please."

She smiled and bit her lip.

"Really? Harry, you're serious? You're proposing to me?"

I looked at her, heart pounding. This wasn't exactly how I had planned to propose to Jean, but it just happened. It felt like the right thing to do at this moment. Life was short. We had no time to waste.

My eyes teared up, and I dropped down on one knee. I was shaking.

"Jean Wilcox...will you do me the honor of becoming my wife?"

She stared at me, mouth gaping, then nodded. Tears sprang to her eyes. Her voice broke as she spoke.

"I suppose there's no harm in that." She sniffled and fought her tears. "Yes, Harry. I would love to marry you."

I rose to my feet, grabbed her in my arms, and kissed her again. As our lips parted, I sighed deeply and looked at Josie and reached for her hand, so she'd feel included.

"This is good. Then the next time there's a pandemic, we'll all be in the same household. We won't have to be kept apart."

Jean gave me a look, with both her eyebrows lifted. Her blissful smile was instantly gone. Both hands landed on her hips.

"Don't you dare talk about another pandemic, Harry Hunter, when we just got rid of this one. I don't even want to hear that word or any other words that have to do with this. Words like *virus*, *social distancing*, and *flattening the curve* are banned for a very long time, do you hear me?"

That made me laugh.

"Loud and clear, my dear. Loud and clear."

THE END

Dear reader

Thank you for purchasing **Never Walk Alone (Harry Hunter#4)**. I hope you enjoyed it.

As I am writing this, we are all in the middle of lockdown due to the Coronavirus or Covid19. There is no cure or vaccine yet, unfortunately.

If I had written this book at another time, before all this craziness happened to our world, it wouldn't have been believable. But now, a lot of these things have become our reality: overwhelmed hospitals, lack of equipment to treat patients, people unable to say goodbye to their relatives, some of them having to do so on FaceTime, all of us being told to stay inside and not socialize. It has truly been a crazy time, unlike anything even I could have imagined.

When I wanted to write another Harry Hunter book, I knew I couldn't just write a normal thriller or mystery in a usual setting. Not with what was happening in the world. There was too much going on around me, and it felt bland —like it didn't really matter. Somehow, I had to incorporate a virus or what is happening in the world right now into my story. I had to write about what I was going through, what we all were going through. I write about the world I am in, and this is our normal now. Who even knows what normal will look like from now on? Hopefully, this won't go on forever, and we'll be able to get back to—if not our old normal, then a new normal—soon enough.

What inspired me to write this book about a new virus, slightly different from Covid19, was actually Reese's story. I read about patient zero in Italy who woke up after three weeks in a coma and had no idea what had happened and how many people he had infected, including his own father, who had since died. The guilt must have been overwhelming. I just knew I had to write about a person who went through what he did, and so it became Harry's sister, Reese's story. If you want to know more, you can read about the Italian patient here:

https://www.theatlantic.com/international/archive/
2020/04/italy-patient-one-family-coronavirus-
covid19/610039/

In the book, I mention Nesera Gesera and how some people believe that this virus was planned and that it is a way to start a total global reset. That is actually not something I have made up. Some people believe in this. There are many videos on YouTube about this, and you can also read about it here:

http://www.blissfulvisions.com/articles/GESARA-
NESARA.html

Also, the bunker where they find Candice and Bobby exists. It's not outside of Miami, but in Mount Dora, also in Florida. And it was actually built by twenty-five wealthy families in the sixties who wanted to survive a nuclear war.

Here's a link to some photos of it and all the amazing information about it (pictures are at the bottom):

https://www.abandonedfl.com/the-mount-dora-catacombs/

Thank you again for reading my books. I hope you're staying healthy and safe. Don't forget to leave a review if you can.

Take care,
    Willow

About the Author

Willow Rose is a multi-million-copy best-selling Author and an Amazon ALL-star Author of more than 75 novels.

Several of her books have reached the top 10 of ALL books on Amazon in the US, UK, and Canada. She has sold more than three million books all over the world.

She writes Mystery, Thriller, Paranormal, Romance, Suspense, Horror, Supernatural thrillers, and Fantasy.

Willow's books are fast-paced, nail-biting page turners with twists you won't see coming. That's why her fans call her The Queen of Scream.

Willow lives on Florida's Space Coast with her husband and two daughters. When she is not writing or reading, you will find her surfing and watch the dolphins play in the waves of the Atlantic Ocean.

To be the first to hear about **exclusive new releases and FREE ebooks from Willow Rose**, sign up below to be on the VIP List. (I promise not to share your email with anyone else, and I won't clutter your inbox.)

Cover design by Juan Villar Padron,
https://www.juanjpadron.com

Special thanks to my editor Janell Parque
http://janellparque.blogspot.com/

———

**To be the first to hear about new releases and
bargains from Willow Rose, sign up below to be
on the VIP List.** (I promise not to share your email with
anyone else, and I won't clutter your inbox.)

- GO HERE TO SIGN UP TO BE ON THE VIP LIST :
http://readerlinks.com/l/415254

Tired of too many emails? Text the word: "wil-
lowrose" to 31996 to sign up to Willow's VIP text List to
get a text alert with news about New Releases, Giveaways,
Bargains and Free books from Willow.

Books by the Author

MYSTERY/THRILLER/HORROR NOVELS

- In One Fell Swoop
- Umbrella Man
- Blackbird Fly
- To Hell in a Handbasket
- Edwina

HARRY HUNTER MYSTERY SERIES

- All The Good Girls
- Run Girl Run
- No Other Way
- Never Walk Alone

MARY MILLS MYSTERY SERIES

- What Hurts the Most
- You Can Run
- You Can't Hide
- Careful Little Eyes

EVA RAE THOMAS MYSTERY SERIES

- Don't Lie to me
- What you did
- Never Ever
- Say You Love me
- Let Me Go
- It's Not Over

EMMA FROST SERIES

- Itsy Bitsy Spider
- Miss Dolly had a Dolly
- Run, Run as Fast as You Can
- Cross Your Heart and Hope to Die
- Peek-a-Boo I See You
- Tweedledum and Tweedledee
- Easy as One, Two, Three
- There's No Place like Home
- Slenderman
- Where the Wild Roses Grow
- Waltzing Mathilda
- Drip Drop Dead

JACK RYDER SERIES

- Hit the Road Jack
- Slip out the Back Jack
- The House that Jack Built
- Black Jack
- Girl Next Door
- Her Final Word
- Don't Tell

REBEKKA FRANCK SERIES

- One, Two...He is Coming for You
- Three, Four...Better Lock Your Door
- Five, Six...Grab your Crucifix
- Seven, Eight...Gonna Stay up Late
- Nine, Ten...Never Sleep Again
- Eleven, Twelve...Dig and Delve
- Thirteen, Fourteen...Little Boy Unseen

- Better Not Cry
- Ten Little Girls
- It Ends Here

HORROR SHORT-STORIES

- Mommy Dearest
- The Bird
- Better watch out
- Eenie, Meenie
- Rock-a-Bye Baby
- Nibble, Nibble, Crunch
- Humpty Dumpty
- Chain Letter

PARANORMAL SUSPENSE/ROMANCE NOVELS

- In Cold Blood
- The Surge
- Girl Divided

THE VAMPIRES OF SHADOW HILLS SERIES

- Flesh and Blood
- Blood and Fire
- Fire and Beauty
- Beauty and Beasts
- Beasts and Magic
- Magic and Witchcraft
- Witchcraft and War

- WAR AND ORDER
- ORDER AND CHAOS
- CHAOS AND COURAGE

THE AFTERLIFE SERIES

- BEYOND
- SERENITY
- ENDURANCE
- COURAGEOUS

THE WOLFBOY CHRONICLES

- A GYPSY SONG
- I AM WOLF

DAUGHTERS OF THE JAGUAR

- SAVAGE
- BROKEN

Contents